Flip
Flop

Flip Flop

WENDY LAWTON

MOODY PUBLISHERS
CHICAGO

All Scripture quotations are taken from the *Holy Bible, New International Version*®. NIV®. Copyright © 1973, 1978, 1984 by International Bible Society. Used by permission of Zondervan Publishing House. All rights reserved.

Library of Congress Cataloging-in-Publication Data

Lawton, Wendy.
    Flip Flop / by Wendy Lawton.
        p. cm. — (Real TV—real transformations series ; take 2)
    Summary: When best friends Briana and Chickie win a spot on the reality television series "Flip Flop," Briana has an opportunity to reveal the terrible secret of her father's alcoholism, and to learn to trust God with the makeover of not just her bedroom, but her family as well.
    ISBN 0-8024-5414-3
    [1. Alcoholism—Fiction. 2. Television programs—Fiction.
3. Interior decoration—Fiction. 4. Family life—California—Fiction.
5. Christian life—Fiction. 6. California—Fiction.] I. Title.

PZ7.L4425Fl 2004
[Fic]—dc22

2004008083

1 3 5 7 9 10 8 6 4 2

Printed in the United States of America

For my friend, Mary Wickstrom

Church Librarian extraordinaire
Her love of books and reading is contagious.

Contents

RealTV

Acknowledgments

Special thanks go to the friends who answered dozens of probing questions for me. If Briana's life rings true, their transparent sharing is the reason. Thank you, Cris, Eileen, Joan, Kathryn, Marie, Sharon, Carrie, Nanette, Glenda, Deb, and Lee.

And, as always, big thanks to the incomparable editorial and design team at Moody Publishers; to my agent, Janet Grant; and to my ever-so-patient family.

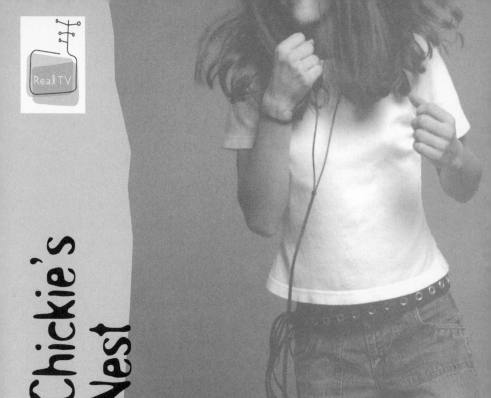

Chickie's Nest

1

Dinner's ready," Mrs. Wells called loudly enough to be heard upstairs in Chickie's room. The simmering smell of homemade spaghetti sauce had been teasing the two hungry girls for the last hour.

"I should go home now," Briana said.

"No. Stay," Chickie said. "Mom always cooks enough."

"I feel funny eating so many meals here . . . ," Briana said, all the while hoping her friend would insist.

"Come on." Chickie motioned to Briana to

follow as she headed down toward the kitchen, taking the stairs two at a time. "Mom," Chickie yelled before she was halfway down, "you don't mind if Briana stays to dinner, do you?"

"Slow down on those stairs, Channing Wells, or you'll end up bumping head over heels all the way to the bottom." Chickie's mom had said those very words for as long as Briana could remember. It never slowed Chickie down, and her mother never seemed to mind.

"Yeah, slow down, *Channing*," Briana whispered, emphasizing the name.

Chickie's mom always insisted on calling her daughter by her given name, Channing. Mrs. Wells often complained that she had picked the prettiest name she could find for her one-and-only daughter only to have that daughter end up nicknamed after poultry.

"And," her mother continued, "I don't mind Briana staying."

Chickie's dad walked into the dining room with his eyebrows drawn together in an exaggerated look of worry. "You mean Briana's not one of our kids? Why didn't someone tell me? I'm afraid I may have mistakenly claimed her on our income tax last year." He took the salad bowl from his wife's hands and put it on the table. "Trish, you've got to keep me straight on these things."

Chickie's mom smiled as she went back to the kitchen.

"Oh, Da-ad." Chickie rolled her eyes. He could be so goofy, but his joking made everything fun. "Don't tease Bree. She worries that she's overstayed her welcome here."

"Can't happen." He turned to Briana. "You do know you're practically part of this family, don't you?"

Briana didn't know what to say. She mumbled an inadequate "Thanks." Her cheeks burned, so she lowered her head to hide the flush. At least she didn't blush as readily as Chickie, whose classic redhead coloration —pale, delicately freckled skin—meant that she could flush from her throat to her ears in a matter of seconds.

That all-too-frequent blush would be worth it if it came with Chickie's carrot-colored hair and russet eyes. Briana was the one who had named the color of Chickie's eyes. "Don't say brown," she always told her friend. "They are so much more than brown. They are burnt sienna . . . terra cotta . . . café au lait . . . russet." Of all those names, russet was the color name that stuck.

Yep. Chickie's coloration always turned heads. Some of their friends insisted that Briana's dark hair, pale skin, and clear blue eyes set her apart as well; but next to Chickie, her combination seemed run-of-the-mill.

"Where are the boys?" Chickie's dad asked.

"Geoff's still upstairs and Sebastian hasn't come home yet," Mrs. Wells said.

Chickie turned and yelled up the stairs for Geoff to come down. Turning to her parents, she said, "I don't know why he needs a personal invitation. We ought to let him starve a time or two."

"Channing, be nice." Mrs. Wells brought in the rest of the meal as Geoff came down the stairs.

"Let's ask a blessing while the food is still warm," Chickie's dad said as they all quieted. He spoke a short prayer and dinner began.

"Did you call your mom, Briana?" Chickie's mom asked. "To let her know you are here?"

"My dad's still out of town, so she decided to work late—month-end." Briana's mom worked as a book-keeper. "She knows if she can't get me at home, she can call me here or leave a message on my cell."

"Your dad is sure gone a lot." Geoff talked with his mouth full of spaghetti.

"Geoff, don't be rude." His mother gave him a disgusted look. "Your comment alone is rude enough, but when it comes with dripping spaghetti sauce, it's more than any of us can take."

Briana jumped in to smooth things over before anyone got upset. "Since you guys say I'm practically part of the family, it's my turn to do dishes tonight."

"No fair!" Geoff whined. "It's Sebastian's turn for dishes. How come he always gets out of it?" At seven years old, Geoff always complained about things not being fair.

"That's sweet, Briana," Mrs. Wells said, ignoring Geoff. "I'm sure Sebastian will be happy to have your help."

The thought of helping Sebastian do dishes conjured up a picture for Briana. Sebastian already attended college since he was a full twenty months older than his sister. When Briana's family first moved across the greenbelt from the Wells' house, Sebastian played with Chickie, Briana, and her older brothers, Michael and Matt. As they got older and Briana's brothers went away to school, Sebastian stopped hanging out with the girls. Now he spent most of his time playing sports and staying busy with college friends.

But Briana never stopped admiring him. In fact, she loved the whole Wells clan, including the very annoying Geoff. *How lucky am I to be able to have a friend like Chickie with a welcoming family like this?*

The Harris family had moved to Mercey Springs in the central valley of California eleven years ago when Briana was six. She and Chickie would be next-door neighbors if not for the greenbelt that ran between their houses. It looked like a strip of park, but it actually collected water into a wash of sorts during rains. It had something to do with conservation or flood control, but Briana didn't know exactly what. She did know it created a parklike space between her house and the neighbors.

The Wells house had a Second Street address. Briana's house was on the corner of Second and Pace, but it faced Pace. As you looked at her house, there were no neighbors to the right either—just a finger of the greenbelt separating the Harris house from the shops on First. It was one of the reasons her parents liked the house. It offered the privacy of a buffer zone all the way around the property.

Of course, Mercey Springs barely qualified as a town. It was just a small collection of vintage houses, a handful of modern housing developments, a few stores, a cardlock gas station, and a Quik-Stop—a typical valley town. Most people lived out in the country on farms or dairies and shopped in Merced about twenty miles away.

The Harrises chose Mercey Springs because it seemed so isolated and somehow secure. Briana's father, a marketing manager for a chemical firm, spent a lot of time on the road, so he wanted to plant his family in what he saw as a safe place. Briana's mom chose the house because there were no immediate neighbors around it. As she always said, she was a private person and didn't want everyone knowing her business.

". . . Mmmm, Mom." Chickie let her tongue run across her bottom lip. "This spaghetti is good."

"It is," Briana agreed.

"Does Briana eat here because they don't got any food at home?" Geoff asked, mouth full again.

"Geoff Wells! What kind of manners are you displaying here?" His mom turned to Briana. "Forgive this boy's atrocious manners. And his grammar." Mrs. Wells shook her head as she repeated, "Don't got any." She looked steadily at Geoff. "He meant to say that he'd be happy to do dishes all by himself tonight to relieve both you and Sebastian."

Chickie started to laugh, but her dad gave her a warning glance before turning his attention to his youngest son. "Geoff, I'm hoping that you were just concerned about our good friend, but comments like that do not belong at our table."

Before Geoff could reply, Briana jumped in. "It's OK, Mr. Wells. I understand curiosity. When I was seven I had all kinds of questions." Actually, now that she was seventeen, she still had all kinds of questions. She'd just learned not to voice them. "Geoff, we do have food, but we don't have anybody at home most of the time to eat it. My house is no fun—not like yours."

Geoff looked embarrassed. "You can come here anytime, Briana."

"Thanks, Geoff. Guess what?"

Geoff looked up from his plate. "What?"

"You and I will do dishes together, and we won't let Sebastian touch so much as a dishrag. OK?" She felt movement behind her.

"And will somebody tell me why I am being plotted against?" Sebastian stepped into the room and lowered his backpack onto the floor near the stairs. He smiled at Briana.

For the second time tonight, she felt a flush creep up her cheeks.

"Hi, Sebastian," his dad said. "Wash your hands and sit down before these guys eat everything."

"Sorry I'm late, Dad, Mom. Practice ran over. It took Coach well into dinnertime to finish yelling at us."

"That good, huh?" Chickie got up to pour milk for him. "At least there's happy news on the home front. Bree and Geoff decided to relieve you of dishes tonight."

"I think I love you, Bree." Sebastian once again turned that gorgeous smile Briana's way. She couldn't think of a single thing to say.

"What about me?" Geoff said.

"Hmmm," Sebastian said as he loaded up his plate. "I do love you, but I have a hard time believing you volunteered."

"Channing, while Briana helps with dishes, why don't you go upstairs and try to muck out your room." Her mom didn't wait for an answer.

"I take it that's not a suggestion?" Chickie asked.

Her mom just gave her *the look.*

Briana loved Chickie's room. The pale colors and airy fabrics made the room feel light and summery. But Chickie kept saying she was tired of it. Lately she barely kept her clothes picked up enough to allow a walkway across the floor.

If I had that room— Bree stopped herself. *Remember the rules. No what-ifs.* She used to waste hours and hours wishing. When she wasn't wishing, she'd be venting. How many times had she gone around her room, around her house and kicked every surface, whispering, "I hate this room. I hate this kitchen; I hate this bed; I hate this . . ." What good had it done? She finally decided to follow the pattern of her brothers and escape.

Of course she couldn't escape to an out-of-state college like they had—at least not yet. Neither brother had come home once since the day they left. They always had good reasons to stay away, even on Christmas.

No, she couldn't physically escape, but she could spend as much time away as possible.

". . . And I don't understand why you don't keep it up like you used to." Chickie's mom must have been talking about her daughter's lack of cleanliness.

"I'm tired of my room. I've had it like that since I was nine."

"Sounds like an eon ago," her dad said with a grin.

"Oh, Dad. How many seniors do you know who still sleep in a white and pink princess bed?"

"How 'bout you, Briana? Do you sleep in a white and pink princess bed?" Mr. Wells turned his smile to her.

"I wish—no, I live in a cave."

"Do you wish you had Briana's cave, Chickie?" he asked.

Chickie shrugged. "I've only seen it once or twice. I can't exactly remember it."

Briana's heart thudded and her breathing began to quicken. *Change the subject. Fast.* "Speaking of caves and fairy princess rooms, if Geoff and I get the dishes done quick and you finish your room, maybe we could squeeze in most of *Flip Flop*." They both loved watching the reality television show where two teens traded bedrooms and, with the help of the show's famous designers, completely redecorated each other's room.

"Good thing I have homework," Sebastian said. "I don't know if I could take another night of teenage decorating angst."

"Good idea, Bree." Chickie jumped up and began clearing the table. "I'll help you clear the table. Let's work fast, and I'll do my room and meet you in the family room in twenty minutes. And just ignore Sebastian. Now that he's in college, he's just too brainy for all of us."

Oh, but those brains are packaged in such a great package. Sebastian's soulful eyes made heads turn, that's for sure. Briana had observed plenty of that head-turning when he was still in high school with them. *Tall, athletic, great hair—moussed and messy—stop. Where are you going with this?*

"C'mon, Geoff. Let's jam," Briana said. "We'll finish clearing the table so your mom and dad can have one more cup of coffee in peace."

As Briana washed the pots, she couldn't help thinking how close she'd come to danger tonight. *Watch yourself. If you get too comfortable, all your secrets may come tumbling out. It's like Pandora's box. Once it's open, you'll never get it all back under control again.*

Flip on the TV, Flop on the Floor

2

I worried that I'd end up watching the show all alone."

Briana put the magazine down as Chickie came flying into the family room.

"My room needed a bulldozer, not a quick cleanup."

"I don't see how you can live like that—it's not like you." Briana kept her room as close to perfect as she could get it. She even color-coded her shirts in her closet. Order and organization —it could have been her middle name. Well, middle names.

"I used to keep it clean, but my room is *so* not me that I can barely stand to be in it anymore." Chickie flopped on the floor and picked up the remote from the coffee table. "I don't get it; you say your room's a cave, yet you still spend so much time cleaning and straightening. How do you make yourself do it?"

Careful, Briana said to herself. *If you go into the reason that order is so important to you, you'll be treading on dangerous ground.* "My cave might be dark and unimaginative, but it's still my little hidey-hole. I like to keep it tidy . . . everything under control." *Now steer her away to other things.*

Talking to herself was nothing new to Briana. She had talked to herself for as long as she could remember, managing to keep a running inner commentary going at the same time as she answered questions and made conversation. She used to wonder if it made her weird, like, mental in some way; but after reading some of the literary novels in senior English, she finally decided she was no weirder than most of the characters. *I wonder if everyone keeps a conversation going inside their mind?*

"You are the control queen, hands down," Chickie said, handing Briana the remote with exaggerated ceremony. "I'm bestowing control of the remote to you."

Briana laughed. "As you well should. Anyone who could have lost her car keys in her own bedroom for an entire week needs a friend who can take control."

"I would have found them. . . ."

Briana raised her eyebrows and mouthed her favorite phrase, "Yeah, right." She turned on the television and scrolled through the channels until she came to the one that carried *Flip Flop.* "Is anyone else going to watch with us?"

"No. Dad's upstairs on the computer; Geoff's in bed; and Sebastian alleges that he's doing homework. Mom took off for some kind of meeting."

As the commercial for a nonchemical wallpaper stripper ended, the *Flip Flop* theme music swelled and the show's opening credits ran—quick vignettes of wild rooms, funny teen antics, and harried designers set into flash-changing multiple screens. The credits always included a few fleeting teasers of the upcoming show.

"Cool. It's not a rerun." Chickie took one of the squishy floor pillows and scrunched it into a ball to prop her up as she wiggled to get comfortable on the floor. The Wells family room practically forced you to get comfy. The couches and chairs were oversized and overstuffed so a person would sink deep into the cushions. The square coffee table dominated the center of the room. Chickie's mom had picked one with a distressed finish so that nothing could harm it further. No one ever worried when the table became littered with soft drink cans, popcorn bowls, board games, or magazines. Mrs. Wells always said she purposely planned the design for their active family—far easier, she said, than trying to redesign the Wells family for a too-fussy room.

"Woo-hoo! It's going to be Claire and Petra," Briana said when she saw which designers headlined the show. She liked Claire's designs much more than Petra's. Her rooms seemed way too wild for Briana. "I pity the poor girl who gets Petra."

"Yeah, but it always cranks up the tension to worry about a design," Chickie said. "Besides, if everyone did classic or pretty, no one would tune in after a while. Half the fun comes from watching outrageous ideas take shape."

The premise of the show was simple enough—two teens, two designers, two bedrooms, two days, two slumber parties, and two checks made out in the amount of a thousand dollars. The teens exchanged rooms and, with the help of their respective designers-in-residence, redecorated their friend's bedroom from floor to ceiling.

"I dig Petra's designs. They're wild and retro." Chickie had been on a retro kick lately. She'd bought the cutest fifties-looking taffeta polka-dot halter dress for the junior prom. It looked like something right out of *I Love Lucy*.

"Not me. I like Claire's light and airy take-me-away kind of designs," Briana said.

"Well, if you like 'take-me-away,' what about Petra's beach bungalow?"

"Oh, kill me." Briana put her hands over her heart. "The turquoise ocean colors were bad enough, but when I saw them carting sand into the bedroom for an indoor sandbox, I couldn't watch."

"Claire doesn't always do light," Chickie said. "I re-member the Out-of-Africa bedroom that freaked out the girl's little brother so badly he refused to step inside."

Briana laughed. "Considering Geoff, would that be such a bad thing?"

"Oh, look at the opener—a rodeo. They must be in Texas."

The opener sequences—the events they called the B-roll—were always filmed someplace nearby to set the scene and give a flavor of the region. It helped set each show apart, since once they got into the actual room re-dos, one room looked pretty much like another. During this segment, the designers; the host, Linley Prior; and the carpenter always goofed around on camera. This time they took turns fooling around with the rodeo clown and a mechanical bull.

"Carpenter Chris is simply too cute to live." Chickie rolled over on her back and hugged the pillow. "How can he have dimples like that *and* be able to work power tools?"

"Can you imagine having a rodeo scene in California? The designers would have to wrestle their way through a crowd of animal rights people carrying protest signs and flinging red paint all over the place." Briana laughed at the picture that made.

"Oh, c'mon. You're making generalizations. Is our part of California like that?"

"Am I wrong that if we were on *Flip Flop*, that's how they'd portray us? In generalizations? California beach girls, Hollywood hopefuls, or wacko political activists."

"I guess that about covers the bases." Chickie laughed. "OK, here's Linley to open the show."

Linley Prior made a joke about a Texas-sized decorating challenge, and then she introduced the two guests. Linley dominated the screen despite her petite size. Her effervescence made the show. Almost overnight she'd become one of the hottest personalities on television.

"I wonder why they never have guys as teen decorators on the show?" Chickie asked.

"They had cousins once, a girl and a guy. Remember?"

"Oh, yeah. But it's usually girls."

"I'll bet that's because it's usually girls who watch the show. Where's Sebastian?" Briana asked to make her point.

"Is that rhetorical or do you wish my hunky brother were down here with us?"

25

Briana threw a pillow at Chickie.

"You're probably right about the audience, though. I'd hate to have to watch a show about a room themed around sports or video games."

The theme music faded once again as the camera panned across two houses and settled on the two girls standing with Linley. "Meet our teen decorators—next-door neighbors, Jill and Ashley." The show's guests swapped house keys as Linley went over the rules. The exciting thing about *Flip Flop* was that the designer and the guest stayed together the whole time, including the night in between the two decorating days. The over-night made it seem like an intimate slumber party. It allowed the camera to get up close and personal.

"Yuck. No wonder that girl wanted a *Flip Flop*. What an ugly room." Chickie made a face as the camera panned around the first bedroom. "My room might be messy, but I can't stand knickknacks all over every-thing."

"She must be the sentimental type. Look at those movie tickets stuck in her mirror and that dried-up chrysanthemum corsage. I'll bet she never threw a sin-gle memento away."

"Shh," Chickie said as she rolled over and pum-meled her pillow back into a comfortable lump. "Here comes the part when the designer asks the teen decora-tor what she wants to create in her friend's room."

"I don't know why the designers bother asking," Briana said. "They already plan to do whatever they want despite the answer."

On the television, designer Petra McLeod sat down next to her teen guest. "So, Jill, what do you think Ashley's hoping for in the way of design?"

The girl named Jill spread her arms wide. "Ash likes cutesy, romantic, pastels—"

"Yeah, right. Like 'Ash' is going to end up with anything close to that," Chickie said.

On the left side of the screen, Petra pulled the girl to the floor near some paint cans. "Pastels, you say?" The camera tightened in on the center can.

"Uh-oh," Briana said. "What do you want to bet it's black?"

The designer smiled straight into the camera as she pried open the lid of the can to reveal a deep red paint. "I guess you wouldn't exactly call this a pastel," she said with mock concern as the shot faded to a commercial break.

"Oh, she's evil," Briana groaned. "You wonder how they usually end up with rooms people love. The designers seem to work hard to give the opposite of what the teen decorators think their friends want."

"If we were on *Flip Flop*, I'd know exactly what to do for you," Chickie said.

"Right," Briana said in a tone that implied the opposite.

"I would. I know you backward and forward. I know everything—everything about you."

"Everything, huh?" Bree smiled, but she couldn't help but think how wrong her friend was. *I wish you knew everything, but you only know what I can let you know.* She sighed. *I'm like that iceberg we saw in* Titanic. *Only the tiniest bit shows above the water. It's the massive underwater formation that's the dangerous part.*

"I know that you like light colors, breezy fabrics, meaningful poetry, and . . . Sebastian."

"Shhh." Briana looked toward the door to make

sure no one overheard. "You are too awful. I like your whole family."

"You can't hide your secrets from me." Chickie twirled an imaginary mustache and made a laugh that sounded like "mua-ha-ha-ha."

If you think that's the extent of my secrets, you know even less than I imagined, my friend.

"Don't give me that knowing look. Chickie knows all, but Chickie tells nothing."

Briana looked at her friend. That much was true. Chickie never shared secrets. Briana had been tempted to tell her everything more than once, but she'd held back.

"Yes," Chickie said with a satisfied grin. "I know more about you than anyone else."

The *Flip Flop* theme music swelled once more, and the paint reveal was repeated in the other house with the other team.

The show continued much like other shows—each teen and her designer worked hard all day, loading out the room, painting, helping make furniture, and resolving any number of minor crises. About halfway through the hour-long show, Day One ended. Each team talked about the homework they'd need to accomplish— usually craft projects—and then they'd get into camera-friendly, comfy sleepwear for the slumber party segment.

It all looked so cozy and intimate—talks about hopes and dreams, design wishes, and life issues. Every now and then Briana had to remind herself that a camera crew followed their every move. *So much for intimate.*

The second day followed. Everything seemed much more rushed. Linley prodded and worried, helped and hurried until everything was finished and the teams did the load-in and all the final dressing of the rooms.

The best part of the show always came at the very end—the reveal—when the girls switched back and got to finally see their own rooms. Both rooms had been transformed and—at least for this episode—both girls loved their rooms. After having watched the entire episode, viewers could see that the rooms fit the teens perfectly, even if they couldn't put words to their style in the beginning.

"That does it," Chickie announced as the last reveal came to a close and the end credits began to run. "I'm applying."

"Applying for what?" As usual, Briana had gotten caught up in the designs and missed many of Chickie's comments.

"I'm signing us up for *Flip Flop*."

Briana couldn't believe what Chickie was suggesting. "How could you do that?"

"It's simple. You just go to the *Flip Flop* Web site, fill out the application, and send a videotape."

"Where would you get a videotape?"

"I've already got a copy of that cooking demonstration we did for Speech—it'll be perfect." Chickie stood up. "Plus, we not only live next door, but we have the greenbelt in between for Carpenter Chris to set up his famous Camp Carpentry."

"They'd never come to Mercey Springs." Briana breathed a sigh of relief that helped slow her thudding heart. *Of course they won't come.* She knew this was true. *Thank goodness.* There was no way they'd ever come to the valley—it was a full hundred miles from the nearest large airport.

"Why not? They've been to Texas."

"Chickie, think. What in the world would they do for the B-roll—film the team's zany antics at the card-lock gas station? I can't think of a single thing that wouldn't be totally lame."

"Maybe you're right, but I can try." Chickie's shoulders slumped. "I'd give anything to get rid of my pink princess bedroom. Seems to me you'd be just as anxious to transform your cave."

"I don't mean to be negative." Briana hated seeing the enthusiasm drain out of her friend. "Of course I'd love to have a designer bedroom." Especially since she knew there was almost no chance of it happening. "Go ahead and try. If they pick us, I'll help you come up with some great ideas for B-roll locations."

Yep. Go ahead and try. If I thought there was any chance at all of getting picked, I'd run the other way. Briana tried to get her heart to slow down. *Talk about Pandora's box— having that kind of scrutiny of my life could blow the lid off my box, and I'd never be able get all the secrets pushed back inside.* She wondered if Chickie could hear the thud-thudding sound. *Please, God, help me keep everything in control for just another year or so until I'm out of there. Please.*

Home Sweet Home

3

Briana slipped the key into the lock of her front door and turned it as slowly as she could until she heard the click of the tumbler. She'd become an expert at opening the door and slipping into her room without making a sound.

Tonight as she opened the door she saw a faint glow of light from the kitchen—the only light in the dark house. *Mom must have left the light on before she went to bed.* Her mom usually went to bed early on the nights Dad worked out of town. Briana moved toward the kitchen to turn out the light before going up to her bedroom.

"Briana." Mom sat at the table, hands folded, waiting. "I didn't hear you come in."

"You're up." Briana's stomach began to tighten. Her mom just sat there. No book, no magazine, no radio—nothing. Briana knew what it meant. "Since you're here, I guess I don't need to turn the light off." Her mouth had gone so dry, she could hear a sort of smacking sound as she said the words. "I'm tired. I'm going up." The words tumbled out. *Weird. If someone listened in to this we'd sound like a normal family. The* Leave It to Beaver *family of Mercey Springs.*

"Your dad said the week's meetings ended badly, and he decided to come home tonight."

See, Leave It to Beaver. *I should jump up and say, "Swell. What time will Daddy arrive?"* Briana turned to walk out of the room, saying nothing more than "Oh."

From of the corner of her eye she caught a freeze-frame image of her mother, still sitting motionless, one hand gripping the other. It made Briana wish she could go put a hand on Mom's shoulder or something, but they never did that kind of thing. You had to be careful not to acknowledge that anything was wrong.

As Briana entered her room, she thought of the *Flip Flop* episode they'd watched tonight over at Chickie's. Escapist TV—that's why she liked it so much. *Chickie thinks she knows everything about me. She thinks she could give me the perfect room.* Briana looked around her room. It was dark. Austere. Not a single thing out of place. The room had no personality. It fit Briana's name for it—the cave. It was a hole. *I think the reason I like a light and breezy decorating style so much is because I long for a light and breezy life—everything out in the open.* She pulled her sweater over her head and reached under her pillow for her flannel pj bottoms and tank top. *Instead I live a huge lie. Oh, yeah, we Harrises look good from the curb, but . . .*

The sound of the automatic garage door interrupted her reverie. *That's a good sign, isn't it? I mean, it takes some form of coordination to find the remote opener and press the button.* Briana strained to listen. She'd become a hands-down genius at detecting trouble long before it even entered her sphere. She quickly finished undressing and getting into her pajamas. *Perhaps if I get into bed . . .*

Crash! The sound of the trash can ricocheting off the garage walls dispelled that notion. Even though she knew it was going to be a long night, she climbed into bed as if everything were normal. *Wait. It* is *normal for me. Forget Beaver Cleaver; this is my life.*

She could hear the sounds of her father stumbling into the house. Silence. She strained to hear. It didn't take long. She heard whispery sounds from her mother followed by yelling.

"Get that kid down here. How many times have I told her to make sure that stinkin' garbage can is out of the way?"

More whispery sounds.

"You stop making excuses for her, Anna." Bangs and slams followed. It sounded like he went into the bathroom. After a minute or so, the yelling started over. "I said, get her down here! I want to talk to her."

"Briana," her mother called up the stairs in a thready voice. "Your father wants to speak to you."

Nothing could be gained by stalling. In fact, the faster she came, the less steam he'd build. "Coming."

She grabbed her robe and headed out the door. *Oops. Slippers.* One time Dad came unglued because she came downstairs in bare feet. He said it showed disrespect. She went back to the closet, got out her fuzzy pink slippers, and slipped her feet into them.

She came into the kitchen. "Hi, Dad." Should she have spoken first? Maybe she should have waited for him to speak. No, if she stood silent, he might accuse her of being sullen.

"I'm gone for a whole week and all I get is 'Hi, Dad'?"

Briana got close enough to give him an air kiss near the cheek. He smelled of hard liquor, not just beer. It was always hard to tell at first exactly how drunk he was. The anger part could be lightly drunk, or it could be the first part of a long series of mood changes if he was thoroughly drunk.

"It's all well and good to stand there meekly." He turned to Briana's mother. "Is there a reason this house is practically dark?"

"No. I mean, yes." Her mother switched on the overhead light. "I thought you didn't want us burning every light in the house."

"Like what I thought ever mattered." He dismissed her with a wave of his hand and turned back toward Briana. "Where was I? Oh, yeah . . . the garbage can. I'm beginning to think you do this kind of thing on purpose."

Briana was lost. *Do what on purpose?* She did not dare ask. Though she could never be sure, silence usually trumped an answer.

"Don't stand there and look at me with that innocent look." He took a deep breath and blew it out through open lips. He looked hard at her, as if searching for something else. "And what are you wearing those stupid slippers for? Do you mean to tell me that when I called you to come down here you made me wait while you put on those ridiculous things? You made me wait after I've traveled hours to get home and just want to get to bed?"

"Brian." Mom put her hand on his arm. "You must be tired. Why don't you go up and get to bed. We can continue this in the—"

He flung his arm up to dislodge her arm. "Don't placate me, Anna. You may let this kid get away with murder while I'm gone, but I have a . . . a responsibility." His words slurred.

Briana stood there without so much as an expression change. When she was little she used to pretend she was invisible, but her imagination had dulled over the years, and pretending no longer worked. She had learned a trick or two that helped her stay as far under the radar as possible. *Don't move any more than necessary. Don't offer any excuses or respond in anything longer than one or two syllables. Whatever you do, don't smile. Don't frown either. Don't fidget. Don't act anxious to leave. Don't look as if you want to stay.*

"Don't stand there looking innocent."

Oops. Forgot the innocent part.

"Just get out of my sight." He dismissed her with a sloppy wave of his hand.

Briana hurried upstairs. Should she take off her slippers for what was sure to be round two? As always, she opted to do nothing. She'd long ago developed an instinct for gauging which action would be more likely to offend and, even though the only thing consistent about living with an alcoholic was the inconsistency, she'd learned to watch faces and try to head off trouble where she could.

She reached under her mattress and pulled out an index card. Long ago she'd carefully copied down a prayer she found on the Internet when she'd searched the words *alcoholic* and *father*. She found pages and pages of sites, but it was the prayer that turned out to be the real treasure. It read:

> God grant me the serenity
> To accept the things I cannot change;
> Courage to change the things I can;
> And wisdom to know the difference.

She'd read those words so many times, she didn't need the card to remember them. Somehow, though, holding the worn card in her hand comforted her. Those were her words: serenity, acceptance, courage, and wisdom. *God, have I come any closer to those things?* She didn't feel courageous tonight. She just felt tired.

She knew she'd achieved some little bit of serenity . . . or maybe she was just resigned. At least she accepted the unchangeable. When she was little her hopes climbed every time her dad promised to quit alcohol forever. Soon she realized it happened after every episode of drinking. It was just part of the pattern. She'd finally learned to accept life the way it was—her dad might feel remorseful and intend to stay sober, but nothing ever changed.

Courage to change—did she have courage to change? *What would I change?* She thought of her mother downstairs. *If I could change one thing, I'd sit down with Mom and talk about the elephant in the living room.* She'd laughed at the thought ever since she heard someone say that in many families alcoholism was like an elephant in the living room. Everyone knew it was there—in fact, they could barely get around it—but no one ever mentioned it.

That's how it had always been in her family. Michael and Matt never said a thing about Dad's alcoholism. They stayed away from home as much as they could during high school and they kept their grades firmly in honor range so they could get scholarships at faraway colleges. When they were still home, Briana felt like instead of a family they were four mostly polite strangers all rooming together. They rarely even made eye contact. Just put one foot in front of the other—that was their motto. Now that her brothers were gone, Dad sent tuition payments and they sent proper thank-you cards. End of relationship.

But courage . . . I wonder if I'd ever have the courage to try to change my relationship with Mom? We may not be able to do anything about Dad, but could we learn to talk together and not just live in the same house? Briana thought about that for a while, but she doubted it would work. Her mother's coping strategy was appeasement. How many times did she ask Briana to do things or not to do things, hoping to appease her father?

"Let's clean the house and make your father a good dinner," her mom would say.

Briana understood the unspoken: *If we are somehow good enough, your dad won't go out and drink.* It didn't take Briana long to see the futility in appeasement. There was no such thing as good enough. If her dad came home from a trip sober, he looked for any excuse to go out and get drunk. The groveling attempts at appeasing him made her dad angrier.

She repeated her prayer under her breath again. "God, grant me the serenity to accept the things I cannot change; courage to change the things I can; and wisdom to know the difference."

The "Serenity Prayer" was the only time she repeated a prayer by rote. It's just that it had come to mean so much to her. She knew God preferred that she talk to Him like a daughter to a father. Well, not her father, but a daughter to a Ward Cleaver-like heavenly father. That's how she usually prayed, but—

"Briana," her father called upstairs. "Baby, come downstairs. Your daddy wants to talk to you." The soft syllables slurred across the consonants, making the words sound sort of slushy.

Dad had progressed quickly tonight. The stages usually took longer. *He must be tired.*

"Coming, Dad."

Sloppy drunk was usually the last stage before passing out. Of course, this was the stage that held the greatest danger of public humiliation. As her father cried and apologized for being the drunk that he was, he was liable to do anything. One time he said he was tired of living a lie, and he started dialing the phone. He had decided to call everyone he knew to tell them what a loser he was. Luckily Matt managed to unplug the phones, and Dad passed out before he could figure out what happened. All they'd need is for her dad's boss and clients to find out about his alcoholism.

If Mom had one goal in life, it was to keep their secret within the four walls of the house. Above all else, including truth, Mom prized a good appearance. So they managed to keep the elephant hidden for the most part. *Who am I kidding? I am the queen of deceit myself. I'll do anything to keep my friends from knowing.* Briana shook her head as she walked into the kitchen for round two. *And Chickie thinks she knows everything about me.*

❋   ❋   ❋

A few hours later, Briana finally settled down to sleep for the night. *Oh, goody. It's only two thirty. I'll be able to get a cool four hours' sleep before school. Typical.*

When she had gone downstairs for the second time, Dad was remorseful and slobbery drunk. He cried and begged her to forgive him. He went through the whole litany—"I'm no good, you'd be better off without me, I never meant to . . . I always intended to . . ." and on and on.

Accept the things you cannot change, she thought as she finally trudged upstairs and let Mom figure out how to get Dad into bed.

Before she turned out the light, she leaned over the edge of the bed and took a metal file and scratched a deep inch-long cut into the wood floor running perpendicular to the baseboard. *Another crisis averted.* She looked at the long line of carved hash marks. *That's not fair. Forgive me, God. I know long ago when I started gouging these marks onto the floor of the cave, it was to show how You'd taken care of me. Thank You, God. And not only have You helped me through, but I've been able to control things so far and keep anyone from knowing anything at all.*

A soon as she prayed that last control part, she felt a funny shiver—almost as if she needed to pay special attention to something. *What?*

Guess What?

4

Don't even stop for an after-school snack, girlfriend. Get over here." Chickie was nothing if not dramatic, but her voice on the phone held something else.

"Now?" Last night had been another crisis night for Briana, and this time she got less than three hours' sleep. Her dad left at noon today for a weeklong business trip, so she looked forward to flopping on her bed and zoning out until dinner.

"Yes, now!"

"OK, OK. But you'd better have a reason. I so looked forward to an afternoon of vegging."

"Just come. Mom wants you to have dinner—she cooked your favorite, pasta primavera. And you know what tonight is, don't you?"

"Oh, that's right. *Flip Flop.*"

"I was starting to worry about you. When you never even mention reality TV the entire day leading up to it, I worry about your health."

"Not my health. I'm losing my grip on reality."

Chickie groaned. "If you insist on making bad puns, you can't come." Before she hung up, she got Briana to agree to hurry over.

Briana left a note for her mom before leaving.

It didn't take much convincing for Chickie to get me to give up my evening alone, Briana mused as she walked across the greenbelt. Dinner at the Wells house always included everything missing in the Harris house. People laughed and joked. Everyone talked over everyone else's conversation. Food reigned and both kids and parents usually lingered at the table.

Chickie met her at the door with excitement dancing in her eyes. What was up? The dinner bustle had already started. Something about the aroma of garlic always enticed the family to gather early. Tonight Sebastian's field practice ended early enough for him to be there in time for the blessing.

Briana sat down at the table, silently chiding herself for noticing Sebastian. *You stop that. Eighteen months, and you are out of Mercey Springs forever with any luck.*

Luck. What a strange word to choose. Once Briana had found Mercey Springs Community Church and started attending with Chickie's family, she learned there was no such thing as luck. People used that word because they didn't know God and they didn't recognize His hand. She knew the truth—luck and coincidence were nothing more than anonymous acts of God.

Mr. Wells asked Sebastian to say grace tonight. He not only thanked God for the food; he thanked God for giving them their mother to cook and care for them. Why did that make Briana feel like crying?

Geoff still talked with his mouth full of food. "Hey, Chickie, did you tell Bree about the let—"

"Mom, make him stop . . . ," Chickie interrupted.

"He just asked a question," Briana said.

"Um . . . he was talking with his mouth full, and totally grossing me out."

Strange. Chickie usually didn't overreact to Geoff's behavior. After all, he was just being seven.

Geoff opened his mouth wide. "You want see-food?"

"Young man." That was all his father needed to say. Geoff slumped his shoulders, cast his eyes down, and closed his mouth.

"It's Chickie's turn for dishes," Sebastian said. "Does that mean Bree's been conscripted again, or can I steal her to read my paper?"

"That's *so* not fair," Chickie moaned. "Last time Bree came, she helped you and Geoff with dishes."

Briana sat doing nothing more than blinking her eyes during the interchange. She couldn't believe Sebastian asked her. "You want me to read your paper? You're in college and I'm only a junior in high school."

"Yeah, but you're a Harris."

Briana looked puzzled.

Sebastian lifted both hands and shook his head. "Don't you know what people say about your family?"

43

Uh-oh, run. Change the subject. Faint. Anything. Briana's heart thumped so hard, she couldn't make a move.

"When you first moved here, people couldn't figure out why you guys stuck so close to home and why you never had piles of kids in your house like the rest of us." Sebastian stopped to take a quick bite of pasta.

Briana couldn't have swallowed if she tried. *Here it comes. All this time I thought my secret was safe. I wonder if I can survive knowing everybody can see our elephant.*

"We thought you guys were weird at first."

"Sebastian . . . ," his dad cautioned.

"No, Dad, we were so wrong. They weren't weird. While the rest of us spent our time goofing around with friends or wasting time on video games, the Harris kids holed up in their house and studied."

Studied? Briana's knees felt weak with a sense of reprieve. *He thinks this is all about super-academics?*

"When college acceptances began arriving," Sebastian continued, "and we heard Georgetown for Michael and then two years later, Duke for Matt, it all made sense."

"So you think we are just studying machines?" Briana smiled. She could live with that.

"I know what kind of grades you get, thanks to my oh-so-talkative sister. Plus, I know how much time you spend in your cave—"

"Thanks, Chickie. It appears my life is an open book." She pretended to be exasperated, but all she could think about was how close they'd come to opening Pandora's box. *Thank You, God. Thank You.* She could live with a family reputation for X-treme geekiness.

"So, how about it, Bree?" Sebastian smiled as he asked. More hardened hearts than hers had melted under that smile.

"Don't you be wheedling my friend away from me," Chickie said, putting her hand on her hip. "We got ourselves a date for dishes and then *Flip Flop*."

Mr. Wells laughed. "Oh, boy, Chickie's got your number, Sebastian."

"How 'bout a bribe?" Sebastian asked.

"I don't need a bri—," Briana started to say.

"I do," Chickie said, laughing. "Whatcha offering?"

"OK. Bree reads and edits my paper, and then she and I go to Cold Stone and pick up ice cream. I'll pay for you, me, and Bree; but if Dad will buy for everyone else, we'll get dessert for all." Sebastian laid his hands on the table palms down. "Deal?"

"You mean if I'll buy, you'll fly?" their dad asked. He loved working worn-out expressions into his conversation. It always cracked the kids up, but this time Sebastian didn't so much as crack a smile.

"Yep." He kept his head low and his eyes focused on his sister—doing his best wheeler-dealer impersonation. "Deal, Chickie?"

"Can you get her home by the opening credits of *Flip Flop*?"

"If we can start on my paper right now. Then it's twenty minutes into town, ten minutes at Cold Stone, and fifteen minutes back."

Mrs. Wells looked puzzled. "Wait a minute. Twenty minutes in and only fifteen back? How do you manage to shave off five minutes on the return trip?"

"It's easy. When you've got ice cream loaded in the car, you take the country roads, even though they're bumpy, in order to keep from meltdown at every signal light."

Mrs. Wells looked worried. "You don't drive too fast, do you?"

"Mo-om! And risk a ticket and increased insurance premiums? I don't think so." He threw up his hands in mock exasperation. "What I wouldn't give to live in an actual city instead of having to drive to the next town to buy ice cream." Sebastian refused to be distracted. He repeated his question. "So, is it a deal?"

"Deal." Chickie high-fived him.

"Ummm, don't I have a say in this?" Briana laughed. She actually couldn't think of anything she'd rather do than help Sebastian and then drive into town with him for ice cream.

"Oops." Sebastian tried to look chagrined. "Miss Harris, would you do me the honor of editing my paper and then accompanying me to town?"

Briana laughed at Sebastian. "Why, certainly, Mr. Wells. Don't mind if I do."

"Are you sure it's OK with your mom, Briana?" Mrs. Wells asked.

"I'll call," Briana said.

"Great." Sebastian picked up his plate and Briana's and took them to the sink. "Mom, Dad, may we be excused?" Before even waiting for an answer, he said, "I'll get my paper and meet you in the family room, Bree."

✳   ✳   ✳

"You seem quiet," Sebastian said as he drove into town. Briana had gone over his paper, suggested a couple of changes, and found one split infinitive and a tense shift.

"I'm facing a dilemma and I can't stop thinking about it," Briana said.

Sebastian glanced over at her and smiled. "Shoot. I'm good at helping people with troubles."

Briana laughed. "This is not exactly trouble; it's a dilemma." She didn't mean to tease, but she couldn't help it. That's what they did together—it was almost a brother-sister thing.

"You can tell me, Bree. We've been friends for a long time."

"OK." She paused. "Do you think it's better to focus on one thing, like, say, vanilla ice cream with crushed Heath Bars, or do a layered creation like brownie, vanilla ice cream, Twix, Snickers, and Skittles?"

He laughed. "OK, I guess I'll learn never to take you seriously."

"This is serious. I haven't even factored in the peanut/almond equation yet."

"You may be high maintenance when it comes to ice cream, but having you go over my paper is worth it to me." He dropped his teasing tone. "Thank you."

"You're welcome, but you didn't really need me. The paper worked. You're really a good writer."

"You think so? I guess it's mostly a confidence thing." He smiled that teasing smile again. "Of course, mostly it was just a ploy to get you alone and to get some ice cream."

Briana just laughed. Being with Sebastian reminded her of the old days when she and her brothers played over at the Wells house. As long as they were away from home, the Harris kids really knew how to have fun together. *I miss Michael and Matt.* Funny, it never occurred to her before. What if she wrote to them and reminded them how much fun they used to have together? *Wouldn't it be great if at least the three of us could stay close somehow?*

"You've gone quiet on me again. I've got a sneaking suspicion this is about more than just ice cream."

"That's not fair. Guys are not wired to be intuitive—you're not supposed to have sneaking suspicions," she said, teasing again.

He laughed but didn't say anything.

Briana realized his concern deserved a straight answer. Sometimes she used teasing to avoid getting close. "I guess being with you reminded me of the fun we used to all have playing together. I miss my brothers."

"I hear you. They don't get home much, do they?"

All the warning signals went off in Briana's head. Being honest to his direct question was one thing, but this could head into dangerous territory. *Change the subject. Fast.* "Oh, here's Cold Stone already. How are you ever going to remember what everyone wants?"

"Silly, that's what I brought you for."

❀   ❀   ❀

"Good timing," Chickie said as Briana hurried in and handed her a partially melted container of ice cream. The commercial ended and the theme music for *Flip Flop* started.

"Phew! We did it in record time." Briana settled in to watch.

"The Alamo?" Chickie wiped ice cream off her mouth as the footage opened on Linley and the two designers riding horses. "They've been in Texas forever."

"I think they stay in one area for a while so they

don't have to do as much traveling. It's been a long time since they did any room makeovers in California, hasn't it?"

"Oh, they're coming soon." Chickie took another spoonful of ice cream.

"How do you know that?" They'd watched every single episode together and Briana never heard a thing about them coming west.

Chickie pointed to her ice cream-filled mouth.

"Oh, right. Since when has a mouthful ever kept you from talking?"

"Oh, look, Bree—guys!" Chickie pointed at the screen. "I can't believe it. They have two guys and two male designers."

"Oh, kill me. So much for my theory that it's basically a girls' show." Briana felt disappointed. "Half the fun is in identifying with the teen decorators. How can I identify with two high school boys? They're practically a different species."

"I know. We'll probably end up with either stereotypical boys' rooms—sports, music, or graphics of some sort—or they'll do a single man's-type place—all chrome and black leather and—"

"I hope this is not a trend. Like they've had all the girl programs; now they'll have all the guy programs."

"Boy, are we prejudiced or what?" Chickie laughed. "Trust me. It's not going to become an all-male show."

Briana looked at her friend. That was the second time tonight Chickie sounded like an authority on the show. Weird. Chickie never acted like a know-it-all. And they watched every episode together. "OK, Chickie, give over. You're holding out on me."

"What? You want the rest of my ice cream?"

"You know what I mean. It's about *Flip Flop.*" Briana narrowed her eyes, trying to look suspicious. "How do you know they're coming to California? How do you know they are not focusing on male rooms?"

Chickie looked downright guilty.

"I know you. You're holding out on me." Briana stood up, stretching every fiber of her five feet three inches as if to intimidate Chickie. She couldn't help tottering a little on her tippy toes. It probably ruined the intimidation factor. Good thing Chickie was still seated on the floor eating ice cream. Her long legs and slim height never allowed Briana a height advantage. "You bought a fanzine on *Flip Flop*, didn't you?"

Chickie started laughing. She set her ice cream down and covered her mouth with both hands to keep ice cream from spattering her friend hovering over her. "That's what you think, huh?"

"Well, if not a fanzine, what, then?"

"Do you really want to know?" Chickie was enjoying this entirely too much. She stretched out every one of those words in an I've-got-a-secret kind of voice.

"No. I guess not. Let's watch the show." Briana acted as if it didn't matter, knowing her friend was dying to tell. She sat back down, pretending to be engrossed in the show.

"You don't want to know?" Chickie couldn't keep the neediness out of her voice. She was dying to tell.

"No. You're entitled to your secrets just as I'm entitled to mine." Briana decided that deep down she must be a cruel person to inflict mental torture on Chickie like this, but it was too much fun to stop.

"Oh, don't start with me now." Chickie folded her

arms across her chest. "You know we don't have secrets from each other."

Bet me.

"What I have"—Chickie held up a business envelope —"is a surprise, not a secret. Don't you want to know?"

"Not if I have to play twenty questions in the middle of *Flip Flop.*"

"You win." Chickie handed over the envelope and waited with a smug expression.

Briana took it and turned it over slowly. A funny sensation in the pit of her stomach hit as she saw the return address. Why would Chickie receive mail from *Flip Flop? Oh, no. Oh, no . . .*

"Aren't you going to open it?"

Briana flipped back the torn flap and slid out a letter. Her hand shook as she unfolded it. "Congratulations," it read, "you've passed the first hurdle on your way to becoming a teen decorator on *Flip Flop.*" Briana's mouth went dry.

"Are you OK? You look like you might faint."

Faint. Yes, fainting would be good. "Water . . ." Briana couldn't speak until she got some water down her throat.

"Just a minute. I'll get you a glass." Chickie ran into the kitchen.

So much for keeping her nightmare under wraps. Briana knew this seriously threatened her ability to keep the Pandora's box of her dad's alcoholism closed. What would she do if the crew came to make over her room and film throughout her house? That type of strain always made Dad drink. In fact, anything out of the ordinary caused him to retreat to the bottle.

But if she refused to go along with the *Flip Flop*

opportunity, Chickie would lose her dream of a *Flip Flop* room makeover. She couldn't do that without an explanation.

All I ever wanted, Lord, was to keep the truth about my messed-up family from coming out. Why does it feel as if I am on a roller coaster headed for a precipice? I can hear the steady click, click, click, click of the car pulling up toward the point of no return, and there is nothing I can do.

"Here. Take a drink. I knew you'd be excited, but I didn't think you'd go catatonic on me." Chickie hovered over Briana like a broody hen over her chick. "Isn't it exciting?"

"I have to say, you surprised me. No question."

"I know." Chickie didn't seem to catch Briana's dread. "I couldn't believe they'd even consider coming to our little hick town, but we made the first cut."

"First cut?"

"Yes. It's not a sure thing. Just a strong maybe." Chickie took the letter, folded it, and slid it back into the envelope. "This little letter is how I knew they were planning to come to California and they have at least one all-girls show under consideration."

"So what's the next step?" Briana felt a wave of relief to find out it was not a done deal. Not yet, anyway.

"They'll send a small film crew out here to shoot our rooms, scout out B-roll locations, and get us on camera to see if we've got the stuff to be stars."

"So if they don't like our rooms, don't like us, or don't like Mercey Springs, they just leave."

"They'll love us." Chickie grinned.

I sincerely hope not. At least we've got a chance that they'll pack up their things and leave forever. Briana looked at Chickie. She could hardly contain her excitement.

"We're going to be on *Flip Flop*. I can just feel it."
Chickie put her arms out and sashayed around the
room, hips in full sway. "We're going be stars . . . we're
going to be stars with gorgeous new rooms."

Jesus, help! Briana took another drink of water.
*What's the chance that I can ever crawl back into my cave
and keep a lid on my Pandora's box now?*

School's over! I can't believe we're finally done with finals." Chickie smoothed out the beach towel before she turned over to sun her other side.

"Do you want me to spread some more sunscreen on you?" Briana asked.

"Hey, why not. I mean, it isn't everyone who sunbathes wearing SPF 40, is it?"

"Well, it isn't everyone who has porcelain skin, russet eyes, natural red hair, and just a sprinkle of freckles." Briana loved the way her friend looked. "What else do you do if you love the feel of warm sun but don't want to peel the rest of the summer? I think you are smart."

"Thanks. Be sure to work some of that sunscreen into my hairline on the back of my neck. I once didn't get it high enough and had such a scalp sunburn that I couldn't brush my hair."

"Eeuuww. Doesn't that gum up your hair?"

"No. It washes right out in the shower." Chickie rolled onto her side and propped herself up on her elbow. "By the way, cute swimsuit."

"Do you like the color?" Briana wasn't too sure about it. She usually liked to shop with Chickie or another friend, but when her mom suggested they get some clothes for summer, she jumped at the chance.

"I love it on you. That hot pink color rocks against your tan skin. With your dark brown hair and light blue eyes, you can wear almost anything, you know." Chickie lay back down on her stomach. "My mom says you have the classic Snow White complexion. Course not now when you have a little tan."

"My mom helped me pick out some summer things the other day when she took a half day off."

"Wow. Your mom? I didn't know you guys ever did girly things together." Chickie swatted at a fly that landed on her sunscreen-slick arm.

"We usually don't, so when she asked me, I jumped at the chance." *Don't tell too much. Go easy here.* "Mom's a quiet, private person. I don't even know her very well. I mean I know her as a mom and I know she loves me, but she never really—well, it's hard to explain."

"I wish she'd come to church with you. I think our moms could be friends. Wouldn't that be too cool?"

"I don't know what she even thinks about church.

She doesn't mind me going." Briana felt uncomfortable talking about her mom—like she was being disloyal or something.

"Well, you could ask."

"I could, I guess." She never really thought much about her relationship with Mom. Was it that life was so chaotic that it hurt too much to open up to Mom? Was it that she somehow resented that her mother didn't do something about Dad? *Who knows? It would probably take a psychiatrist half a lifetime of listening to me to figure out what's broken here.*

Chickie propped herself up on her elbows, pulled out a magazine, and began to read.

"You better put on sunglasses, or the sun on those shiny pages will burn your eyeballs," Briana warned.

"You sound like my mother, not my best friend."

Briana went back to thinking about Mom. What if she didn't try to figure out why their relationship was so weird? What if she just tried to make it a little better? That wouldn't take a psychiatrist. *I mean, what if I just get it 10 percent better so we smile at each other in the morning? Or what if I try to do something little every day to reach out?*

It worked with Michael and Matt. That night she'd gone for ice cream with Sebastian, she decided to write to them, and she did it that very week. In the letter, she reminded them of the fun they'd had playing with the Wells kids on the greenbelt. Michael wrote back right away, asking lots of questions about her, telling her a little bit about his life at school, and he ended with, "Take care of yourself, kid." Briana read and reread that letter until the paper began to split along the fold lines. She wrote back and had already received another letter.

Matt took a long time to reply. His letter seemed more guarded, but Briana figured it was a start anyway. What if she tried to reach out to Mom in some small way? *Jesus, help me pick the right thing to do.* And she wouldn't be doing all the reaching—her mom's offering to take her shopping was a total surprise. They felt a little shy with each other, and they never talked about Dad; but her mom really helped her pick out cute things, and they even had lattes afterward.

"Oh, those kids with the football are so not coming out here on the greenbelt to play, are they?" Chickie shaded her eyes with her hand as she looked off in the distance.

"You didn't think we'd have it to ourselves for long, did you?" Briana began gathering her things together. "Besides, I think I've had enough sun."

"Channing?" Her mom stood on the front porch and called. "Telephone. Sounds important."

Chickie jumped to her feet. "Important? Bree, this could be it." She began running toward the house. "Oh, wait. I don't want to sound breathless." She slowed down. "Could you get my towel and the magazines and the sunscreen and—"

"Go! I'll get everything." Briana slowly gathered everything together. Flip Flop *on the phone, no doubt. With my luck*—she stopped that thought midway. *There I go again with that "luck" thing. There is no such thing as luck. But if it's not luck—if it's God doing all this—I don't even want to start with the why questions. They'd go on forever. No wonder people prefer to believe in luck.* She could almost hear the *click, click, click* of the roller-coaster car again. There could be no getting off, that's for sure.

"It took you long enough," Chickie said as Briana came into the kitchen with all their stuff.

"You're already off the phone?"

"Yep. Guess what?"

Briana squinted her eyes and gave Chickie the look that said *don't do this to me again*.

"OK, OK." Chickie put her hands out, palms down, fingers splayed as if to try to tamp down the excitement. "That call was from Derek Samuelson, director and producer of the award-winning television show, *Flip Flop*." She screamed and jumped up and down.

Jesus, please, help me. Briana couldn't think of a thing to say.

When Chickie finished doing her version of the happy dance—which included jumping up and down, stirring the pot, and a few Macarena moves—she looked at her friend. "You do know what this means, don't you?"

"I take it that we're going to the next step." Briana tried to look happy.

"How can you be so calm? Mom ran upstairs to call Dad."

"I must be in shock." What could she say to her friend? She didn't want to bleed off any of the excitement, but for her, this was the worst thing that could happen. "Give me a couple of minutes to let it sink in."

"They pull in here on Monday to do a sort of screen test—on us, on our houses—I guess on Mercey Springs as well. It'll be Linley and a cameraman. They'll take all the raw footage back and make their decision." Chickie closed her eyes and breathed deeply through her nostrils. "Is this cool or what?"

"You're amazing, Channing Wells," Briana said. That much she could say in all honesty. "The fact that you managed to get us this far is nothing short of incredible." She hugged Chickie. "You know what I need to do? I need to go meet my mom at work and break the news to her."

"You mean you haven't told your mom yet?"

"It seemed such a remote possibility, and she's such a private person. I didn't want to worry her for nothing."

"What if she says no?" Chickie pulled away.

"She won't say no." Briana knew this for a fact. Her mother tried to make everyone happy. "I just need to tell her. I'll call you this afternoon, OK?"

"Good. We need to talk strategy, clothes . . . I mean, there's so much!"

❋   ❋   ❋

"Mom? Can I take Dad's car and drive up there to take you to lunch?" Briana said into the phone.

Her mom was silent for the longest time. "Sure. Can you give me until about one? Then I can get this account reconciled and be less pushed for time."

So Briana drove into Modesto and parked in a downtown lot near her mom's building. She walked around for about fifteen minutes waiting for one o'clock when she went in and had her mother called down to the reception desk.

"Hi, Mom. You ready?"

"Sure." She turned to the receptionist. "Maggie, this is my daughter, Briana."

Briana put out her hand, smiled, and greeted the woman before turning back to her mom. "Shall we go to that new café with the tables right on the street?"

"Sure, honey. Whatever you want." Her mom seemed to be searching her face. "Your call surprised me at first. Then I thought, why shouldn't we meet for lunch? I don't know why I'd never suggested it."

Once they'd ordered, her mom leaned in a little. "Did you have a specific reason for coming up here—not that you have to have a reason, but—I mean . . ."

"I guess I have two reasons. One long overdue and the other a crisis of sorts."

"Well, why don't you give me the overdue one first, and we'll get that out of the way before we tackle the problem."

Briana realized that might have been the longest conversation she'd had with her mom in a long time. "OK. Long overdue. I've begun to realize that because of the problems . . . well, you know, I've kept myself apart from you. I want to try to change that, Mom."

Her mom didn't say anything. She just sat there with one hand gripping the other. The waitress came and delivered Briana's Pepsi and her mom's water. Just as Mom seemed about to speak, the waitress came back with a question about the order.

Is this how the conversation will end? In the past, we've never confronted anything head-on. In fact, we rarely made eye contact.

"It's not you who needs to change." Her mom seemed to pull the words from somewhere deep down inside. "I don't want the distance anymore either, but . . . I don't know . . . there's so much I wish I did differently; and yet, I don't know how to change things."

"You mean about Dad?"

"I can't even bring myself to talk about it. It's just that . . ."

"I know. I read that alcoholism is like an elephant in the middle of the living room. Everyone walks around it, but nobody mentions it."

"Don't say alcoholism," Mom said in a whisper. "Yes, your dad has a problem with drinking sometimes; but he holds a responsible job, never misses a single trip, makes an excellent salary—"

"It's OK, Mom. I can say 'drinking problem' instead." Briana also kept her voice down, knowing how sensitive Mom was.

"I guess it sounds silly to worry about what we call it, doesn't it?" Mom unclasped her hands and took a drink of water.

"No, not to me. I've learned to be very careful and to keep everything inside. I'm the queen of secrecy. That brings me to my problem." Briana took a drink and waited for the waitress to set their plates in front of them. "Chickie knows nothing about my life. That's why I never have friends over."

Mom sighed and looked like she wanted to say something. Instead she took her fork and pushed a salad leaf toward the middle of her plate.

"I told you about *Flip Flop*, right?"

"The television show you and Chickie watch?"

"Yep. Remember, you and I caught part of a rerun one time?"

Her mom nodded as she took a bite.

"Well, a while back, Chickie wrote to the show and submitted our names as possible show guests."

Mom put her fork down and folded her hands. "And?"

"They wrote first and then they called. We made it past the first hurdle, and now they are coming out next

Monday to look at Mercey Springs, look at our rooms, and give us a sort of screen test."

Mom still sat there, just like she sat all those nights waiting for Dad to come home.

"Mom, I never thought it would get this far. I mean, what are the chances? I didn't stop Chickie because I didn't know what I could say—what I could tell her as my reason." Briana knew she was prattling on without any idea where she was going with this.

"Your fries are getting cold. I'm going to need to let this sink in." Her mom took another bite and chewed slowly. "Next Monday, and Tuesday even, are no problem. You dad will be in Oregon. It's too far to come home on a whim."

Briana continued eating, but she realized this was the first time her mother had ever addressed the problem head-on.

"I'm not ready to confront your dad about this. I mean, when he's not been drinking, he'd be delighted and think it a lot of fun."

Briana realized she never thought of her dad sober. Most of his sober hours were when he was working, so they happened away from home. She realized that most of her mother's time with her dad must've been sober times until more recent years. Funny. No wonder her mother could think of his alcoholism as a temporary bump in the road.

"What I need to do is approach this in a problem-solving way, like I'd do at work." Her mom seemed to be thinking out loud. "I want you to be able to save face and have this experience. Let's just take it a step at a time." She reached across the table and gave Briana's hand a quick squeeze. "We're OK for this first test. I'll make sure to get the day off."

"So you'll be around?" Briana felt as if a weight had been lifted off her.

"I'll make sure I am. If you two are chosen to go farther, we'll just have to work something out. Let's take one step at a time."

They finished eating and talked about their surroundings, Mom's work—everything but the elephant. That was OK. Briana knew this, too, needed to come one step at a time.

"I'm so glad you called and we did this. Thank you." Her mom took the check.

"I'd planned to treat you, Mom."

"You did, but you're not paying. The treat was in being together."

"I know. It makes me wonder why we allow distance to come between us. It's like Michael and Matt—" Briana stopped when she saw the look of pain cross her mother's face.

"What about Michael and Matt?"

"I'd just let them walk out of my life until one day I thought about them and felt lonely. I decided to do something about it. Kind of like I decided to do something about me and you." Briana took her napkin off her lap and put it on the table.

"What did you do?" Her mother leaned in again. Briana noticed she did this every time the subject really mattered to her.

"I wrote to them."

"Just like that?"

"Yep. And they wrote back. In fact, Michael's written a few times. Mom, we're slowly rebuilding our friendship."

"Just like that." Mom seemed to be talking to herself. She took her napkin and touched the outer corner of her eye. "Could I read the letters sometime?"

"Sure. Anytime." Briana wondered again how her family wound up so alienated from each other. "Mom, why don't you just write to them? You don't have to go into anything heavy—just write." Briana smiled. "One step at a time."

As she drove home, she couldn't stop thinking how glad she was that she called her mom. Actually, it was the *Flip Flop* crisis that started her on this path. *Interesting* . . . And it looked like things were OK for this first screen test. The Pandora lid could stay tightly closed. *Now all I have to do is figure out how to be dull enough so that Linley decides to move on.*

❋   ❋   ❋

"Channing, why don't you take us up to see your room?" Linley Prior spoke right to the camera. As soon as the camera stopped rolling, she asked, "You signed your letter 'Channing,' but everyone calls you Chickie. Which do you prefer?"

"My mom prefers Channing, but I'm really Chickie." Mrs. Wells threw up her hands in resignation.

"Then Chickie it is." Linley was every bit as pretty in person as she was on television. "Why don't both of you girls come upstairs and give me the tour of Chickie's room?" She turned to the cameraman. "Since we're using raw footage to show Derek, you can cut the camera off when we're moving from place to place. I want to get some of the spontaneous stuff, but with no editing, it could be impossible. Just edit with your on/off switch, OK?"

Briana had no idea when the camera was on and when it was off. Stress time. She walked a tightrope here. She wanted to support Chickie, but she wanted to come off dull enough on camera that they'd pass over Mercey Springs. Problem is, she didn't want Chickie to catch on. *Here I am again, the queen of deceit.*

"Roll. So this is your room, Chickie? Tell us what you'd like to see changed."

Chickie smiled as she flicked the curtains. "There's not much in here that I don't want changed. We did the room when I was between Pretty Ponies and Barbie. The princess furniture, the pink carpet . . . I mean, look at me. Do I look like a pink sort of girl?"

Linley laughed. "Are you saying you wish your room reflected your autumn amber tones?"

"I wish my room reflected anything other than as-seen-on-TV tweeny-bopper toy mania." Chickie shuddered visibly.

Briana could see that the cameraman loved the way Chickie came across. He moved in to get different angles and adjusted his lens.

"Briana loves my room, don't you, Briana?"

The camera panned over to Briana. "Um, yeah." She had to add something else or Chickie would get suspicious. "I've always been a Pretty Pony sort of girl, but keep that on the down low, would you? It's bad for my image." She kept her face expressionless even though she decided to look directly into the camera to make sure the director got the full effect of her thuddingly dull personality.

"So, Bree, what would you see in this room?" Linley asked.

"Most of the time the room needs a bulldozer."

"Briana!" Chickie whacked her on the shoulder.

"So, you're saying we need to address storage." Linley smiled. "Great suggestion. What about colors?"

Briana drew a blank at first. She looked at Chickie, standing there with such a hopeful look in her eyes. "Russets, maybe terra cotta, warm . . ."

"Sounds like she's describing you, Chickie," Linley said.

"Can you see why she's been my best friend ever since she moved almost next door? She always sees me in the most flattering light." Chickie looked right at Briana.

Briana couldn't help herself. She reached out and hugged her friend. *Rats. So much for passive.*

"OK. Let's go take a look at Bree's room." Linley helped the cameraman gather his cases, and they headed downstairs and out the front toward the Harris house.

"This is our greenbelt," Chickie said, sounding like a tour guide. "We thought it might be a great place to set up Camp Carpentry."

"Jack, you're rolling, right?" Linley asked. When he nodded she said, "Great! I've never seen a better setup for us to work. Be sure to pan from one house to the other so we can get the scope, the relative isolation, and that lovely, lovely greenbelt. Plus, these houses are so pretty—vintage."

Briana's stomach began to tighten.

"What about a place to set up the sewing center?" Linley asked. "We set up just one center, and both teams take turns. What's your garage like, Bree?"

"There's nothing in it but two cars and a garbage can. My dad likes it to be empty for the most part. We store our tools outside in the shed, and bicycles are hung on hooks on the wall." Briana didn't tell her that they kept it empty to keep her dad from breaking his neck when he stumbled into the house. "It doesn't have much light, though." There, that should be a big drawback.

"No problem. We bring lights and extra generators, just in case. The hardest thing to find is uncluttered space. Jack, can you see how perfect this could be?"

Briana's mom met them at the door of the house, inviting everyone inside. Once introductions were finished, they headed upstairs.

Linley stopped on the landing. "What an exquisite quilt. Is someone here a quilter?"

Mom spoke up. "I used to quilt. That's one of mine."

Briana didn't know that.

"Can you sew as well?" Linley asked.

"Yes."

"Perfect. I know it looks like the designers and the teen decorators do all the work themselves, but it would never be possible. We bring along a sewing co-ordinator, Suzanne Maher, but we like to hire an assistant locally." Linley turned to Mom again. "If we come to Mercey Springs, could you be available for the day before and the two actual days of the *Flip Flop*?"

"I think so. I work in accounting, so as long as it isn't month-end, I should be all right." Briana's mom seemed almost enthusiastic.

"You mean it's not like we see on TV? Two people doing every single thing?" Chickie looked stricken.

Linley laughed. "Much of the work is done by the actual designer and teen, but, no. We bring our carpenter—"

"Right. Carpenter Chris," Chickie said.

"He's our on-camera carpenter, since he's mighty fun to look at." Linley smiled. "I hope the camera's not running, Jack."

"You're hoping I'm not collecting blackmail bait, huh?"

Linley gave him a tiny punch to the shoulder. "Anyhow, we bring a master carpenter, Joe, with us as well, though you never see him on camera."

Briana had to laugh at the expression on Chickie's face. "Reality bites, huh?" Briana asked.

"We will also need to hire a helper for Camp Carpentry. Any strong guys around here?"

"My brother, Sebastian, likes working with power tools and is on break from college," Chickie offered.

"Again, perfect. OK, Briana, take us up to this famous cave of yours."

The reality hit. Briana walked upstairs. She couldn't believe she consented to bring a houseful of people into her private world. She often wondered if the room had somehow absorbed the apprehension, the hours of waiting for the next onslaught, the hopelessness. *Stop being overly dramatic. It's just an ugly room.*

"So this is your room?" Linley said. "The cave, right?" She walked around and motioned to the cameraman to follow her. "It's dark . . . almost atmospheric, but the room is big and the proportions are wonderful—high ceilings, gorgeous craftsman woodwork." She stopped and turned to face the camera. "Tell us, Bree, what do you wish you could have in here?"

Before Briana could speak, Chickie jumped in. "Not Pretty Ponies and Barbie. That's for sure." Everyone laughed.

"I love light." Briana surprised herself. She hadn't meant to be quite so honest. *Oh, well, I may as well continue. If we do happen to win an episode with this screen test, I'd rather get a room I love than go through all this for*

something in chrome and leather. "I'd like to see light curtains blowing into the room. Fresh air. There's a gigan-
tic old lilac bush outside that reaches up to the second
story. In the spring, I'd love to throw the windows open
and let the room fill with the scent of lilacs. I'd like
white linens on the bed that smell like they've hung on
the line in the sunshine." She looked over at Mom. Did
Mom wish for the same cleansing wind to blow all the
secrets out of their house?

"Wow," Linley said. "You can make us see the design
in words alone." She turned toward the cameraman. "I
think we have enough. Let's wrap up here, and then
we'll scout the area to see if we can find some interesting locale for our B-roll footage."

When the girls helped get the equipment out to the
car, Linley thanked them for participating. "We'll be
back in touch within a week."

A week. Briana felt so mixed up. How she wished her
life were uncomplicated enough to be able to hope for
a positive call. Whatever the outcome, there could be
no turning back. With a little luck—no—with God's
help, perhaps she could keep the lid on her Pandora's
box long enough to get through whatever came their
way.

*Funny. Why do I get a troublesome feeling that maybe
God isn't as concerned with keeping the lid on all our secrets?*

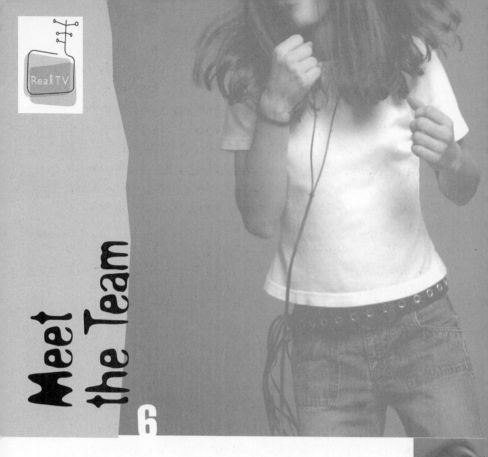

6

Briana woke to hear knocking at her door. Banging, actually. Yikes! What if it woke Dad? He came home last night and it was one of *those* nights.

She ran downstairs to get the door before the commotion could penetrate her father's sleep. That was silly. He'd probably only been asleep four hours. Last night had been a slobbery, re- morseful session. He'd sleep until dinner.

"Chickie! What's wrong?" Her friend stood there in a pair of Sailor Moon flannel pj bottoms and a tank top. "Come in before someone arrests you for indecent exposure."

"What do you mean, indecent? Kids wear this to school."

"Don't remind me. It's not exactly a fashion statement." She closed the door and led Chickie into the family room.

"So what brings you to my doorstep so early on a summer vacation morning?"

"I've got news and I won't even make you guess." Chickie grabbed her hands. "We're in! They loved us. Derek Samuelson called today and gave us three possible dates."

"We're in?" Briana heard a door close upstairs. She immediately felt a tightening in her chest. "Just a minute. Let me run upstairs for a minute. I need to check something. I mean, my dad got home so late and we didn't get to bed until, well, early this morning; and it can't be my dad who's awake, and so I need to check . . ." She knew she sounded like an idiot. "Wait."

She ran upstairs to find her mom in the hallway. "Oh. I heard a noise and I thought—Chickie's here with news. I thought you'd gone to work and—"

"No, I just couldn't get up this morning." Her mom gave her an awkward hug. "I can guess what Chickie's news is. Congratulations." She and her mom were not normally physical with one another, but since their lunch they had been more aware of each other and were both trying hard. "And don't worry. We'll figure this out."

Briana tiptoed back downstairs. How she wished she could be sure that her mom would figure it out.

"It was my mom," Briana said to Chickie as she

walked back into the family room. "I thought she'd gone to work, but she's a little under the weather."

"So are you excited?" Chickie asked.

"I'm excited and scared." Briana wondered what made the director choose them. "What did Mr. Samuelson say about our screen test?"

"Remember how stilted you were at first?"

Stilted. That's an interesting word. "It's not too easily forgotten."

"Well he said he loved our 'synergy.' That was the word he used. He said I was effervescent and it might have been 'over the top' if you hadn't balanced it with an understated, droll sense of humor. Those were close to his exact words."

Briana laughed. She couldn't help herself. *You really crack me up, God. I tried so hard to be dull and uninteresting in order to get out of this. Had I just been my normal self, we would have been what Mr. Samuelson called, "over the top" I give up.*

"You're laughing. So that means you're as happy as I am, right?"

"Oh, Chickie, I don't think anyone can be as happy as you are about this."

"OK, we've got work to do." Chickie took out a Hello Kitty notebook and started writing.

Briana put her hands on her hips, pretending to be exasperated. "What is that?"

"What?"

"We're worrying about redoing your pretty pink princess bedroom into something earthy and sophisticated, and here you come, bopping over here in Sailor Moon pj's with a Hello Kitty notebook? I'm beginning to think your room is already perfectly Chick-i-fied."

Briana laughed at her friend until she remembered her father upstairs. "Come on outside before my snickering wakes my poor family."

They settled on the bench at the edge of the greenbelt. "This is good," Chickie said. "It gives us the wide-angle view of our two houses. Great for planning."

"As long as you're OK with the town having a wide-angle view of you in your pj's . . ."

Chickie ignored her. "It's going to be too cool to have the greenbelt filled with Camp Carpentry."

"I still can't believe it." The odds of something going wrong grew every time Briana pictured this. No way could they get through this without her father knowing. For someone who tried to exist well under the radar, this was practically making her break out in hives.

The worst thing that could happen would be to have him get caught up in the excitement and decide to be around during the filming of *Flip Flop.* He'd start out with every intention of being sober—how many times had he talked about wanting to be the best dad? But if a problem came up, or if he didn't get enough sleep, or if someone made him mad, or if someone overlooked him—he'd either sit down with a bottle "just to take the edge off," or he'd head into a neighboring town to drink in one of the clubs. Afterward he'd erupt and stage a scene—and not the made-for-TV kind of scene.

If he stayed home intending to stay in the background, he'd end up feeling left out, wander into town, and—well, the scenario never varied. The only thing that would allow Briana to get through this with secrets intact was if her dad had a business trip that lasted the whole time. *Please, Jesus . . .*

"I can't believe it either. You seem so quiet. Are you

like me? Picturing how everything is going to work?" Chickie swung her legs back and forth. "When kids from school find out that Carpenter Chris is going to be here right on our greenbelt—tool belt and all—it'll be a circus."

Briana felt that hollow feeling in her belly again. *Yeah, baby. The Harris family unravels—not just in front of the biggest audience on cable television, but also in front of the entire Mercey Springs High School.*

"Wanna know a secret?" Chickie smiled in that conspiratorial way. "Sebastian started worrying about having to work in a fitted *Flip Flop* T-shirt next to Carpenter Chris. He's started going to the weight room at school every day."

"Oh, I bet he'll really appreciate everyone knowing that. I think I'd keep that one on the down low." *See. Everybody is already freaking out.*

"I wouldn't tell anyone else, but it was too good to keep to myself." Chickie opened her notebook and got back to business. "My mom was going to call your mom at work to help choose the day since so many people have to be coordinated. Shall I tell her to call at your house today instead?"

"Let me get back to you on that. My mom may go to work in the afternoon."

"The *Flip Flop* team will be coming to do a one-day location test for the B-roll shoot. They've planned it so we can meet the designers and they can scope out our rooms."

"They're coming all the way here just to meet us and then go back?" Briana didn't even know where "back" was.

"No. It's just like we suspected. They group shows

together regionally. They'll come up here either before L.A. or before Monterey—whichever works out."

Briana was impressed. "You've really done your homework."

"You should see the fanzines available, not to mention books," Chickie said. "Did you know that unless there's a break or a holiday, the designers don't get to go home until the season's over? Weird. Can you imagine being away that long?"

What are you talking about? Does that sound so bad? Briana rubbed her eyes. How many hours of sleep did she get last night? She was beginning to get punchy.

"Do you know that, after the designers have taken measurements and shot photos of our rooms, they'll sketch designs and do room plans during breaks in other shows?" Chickie knew the drill. No question—a new reigning queen of *Flip Flop* trivia was born.

"So they buy the fabrics and supplies on the road?" Briana asked.

"Uh-huh. For our episode, they'll either shop in L.A. or Monterey."

"Cool." The logistics of doing show after show boggled the mind. "Pity the poor teens who follow us. The designers will have to shop for their rooms out here in the boonies." She laughed at the thought. "Face it. The next episode will feature a *tres chic* black-and-white design in a Happy Holstein motif."

"OK. We've got work to do." Chickie went back to her notebook and put a check in the lopsided box she'd made beside her entry about the moms and scheduling. "Now, onto serious stuff—hair, nails, and fashion strategy."

"I don't want to be a downer, but won't our hair be

twisted up out of the way in a clip? And won't we be wearing the famed *Flip Flop* T? And—"

"If you're going to say anything about not needing our nails done because of sandpaper and paint, I'm going to have to pull your official membership card in the universal sisterhood of the female of the species."

"I'm not saying a manicure wouldn't be nice—"

"Nails are a nonnegotiable in this situation." With exaggerated precision, Chickie put her thumb and forefinger together and raised her hand up in front of her face with a flourish as if she held an imaginary cup.

"What? We're going to be drinking tea? I've never seen that on the show."

"Bree, for someone purported to be so smart, you are uncommonly dense. Think! The key?"

"Oh, the key swap. Got it." The ritual that began each show was the introduction of the two teens and the swapping of house keys. "But you are going to get a professional manicure for a thirty-second shot of one hand in motion?"

"No. You didn't understand. *We* are going to get professional manicures for a thirty-second shot of *two* hands in motion."

❋　　❋　　❋

That marked a turning point for Briana's summer. Shopping and planning consumed whole days. Even though both girls had long hair, they each had the ends trimmed and deep moisturizing treatments applied from roots to ends. Chickie had read a piece about cameras loving shiny hair. Shopping for jeans took multiple trips. Chickie insisted the pants fit perfectly, yet bend and move easily. It was a good thing Briana squirreled away her Christmas and birthday money.

The whole thing would've sent Briana over the edge except that it helped take her mind off the constant worry about her father and what might happen when their carefully orchestrated world was flip-flopped. Without the distraction of Chickie's excitement and the constant planning, her daytime tension level might have been as bad as her night worries.

She enjoyed the days of preparation since they were less about the show and more about her friendship with Chickie. She guessed this might be the last summer they had together. After all, graduation loomed in less than eleven and a half months.

When the day came for them to meet the team, they were practically twitchy with excitement.

"I wonder which designers we'll get," Chickie asked as a black SUV turned the corner. "It looks like they're here."

"Oh, look." Briana pointed toward the second car. "It's Claire Hewitt and Petra McLeod."

Derek Samuelson got out of the driver's seat and unpacked a few things. He took two folding tables and several folding chairs from the back of the SUV and set up a temporary conference room right there on the grass about halfway between the two houses. Derek took charge immediately, inviting everyone to sit down. He stood, focusing on Chickie first. "I know you from the screen test. You're Channing Wells. How do you do?"

Chickie shook hands with him.

"Do you have any idea how much the camera loves your coloration?"

His comment caused her to blush to an even deeper coloration.

"And you must be Briana Harris. How do you do?" He put his hand out to her as well. "You were great in the test. Your understated humor and reserve worked perfectly on camera."

"Thank you." Briana wished she could get out of this. The director exuded confidence and organization. How would he react to an out-of-control chaotic scene in the middle of his taping?

"OK, we need both sets of parents. We have a stack of papers to sign before we can even begin."

"Mr. Samuelson, this is my mom. . . ." Chickie made the introductions as the designers came walking up. They stopped and Mr. Samuelson made introductions all around. It must have been confusing to the *Flip Flop* team, but Briana knew most of them from the show. Mr. Samuelson insisted they call him Derek. Everyone else agreed—it was to be first names.

With the formalities out of the way, Briana spoke up again. "Derek, my mother is here, but my father is on a business trip. Can she sign the papers alone?"

"Anna, right?" he asked, addressing Briana's mother. "Are you listed on the title to the house?"

"Yes."

"Good. No problem, then." He handed a stack of papers to Chickie's parents and a stack to Briana's mom. "Now, I understand several of you are willing to help out during the filming. Let's see . . . Sebastian, are you here?"

"I'm Sebastian Wells." Sebastian stepped out and shook hands with Derek.

"Good. You've agreed to assist the carpenters, right?"

"Right."

Derek took a small stack of papers and handed them to Sebastian. "You probably won't appear on camera, but we'll pay you scale for local talent with a stipend for skill level. You need to fill out this form for taxes, this one for insurance, this one for—well, it's all self-explanatory."

He repeated the process with Briana's mom, who planned to take vacation from her regular job so she could help run the sewing machines in her garage.

Derek continued the meeting. "One problem we came up against here in Mercey Springs is the lack of a caterer who could do all the meals for a crew our size. Linley told me about the delicious lunch she was served at the Wells house when she came to film the test." He paused in his machine-gun-delivery style. "This is a little out of the ordinary, but we were wondering if you two would be willing to cater three meals for all three days— Day Zero, Day One, and Day Two. You could do it right on the greenbelt here. We should have room to set up a temporary canteen right next to Camp Carpentry."

Mr. and Mrs. Wells looked surprised but seemed interested. "We couldn't do a professional catering job, but we've cooked plenty of times for large crowds at church," Mrs. Wells said. "And Nick's renowned for his barbecue skills."

"You wouldn't have to cook every meal. You could contract with several small caterers if you'd like, but it would help us to have someone take charge."

"I think we can do it," Mrs. Wells said.

"Thanks, Trish. We may look like a big organization on television, but we're actually a small, tight-knit, hardworking team. We rely on local talent to fill in the gaps. There will be ten of us—Linley, two cameramen, one assistant, the two designers, two carpenters, one seamstress, and me. Add the members of both your families and you have the meal count. We pay a per-meal, per-person stipend. It's pretty generous."

"Sounds great. Plus, it'll be lots of fun," Mr. Wells said. He looked over at his youngest son, who hadn't come to the table, but stayed back by the bushes. "Geoff can do KP."

"Will I get paid?" Geoff asked, stepping closer to the table.

"You betcha. Of course we'll pay you," his dad said. "You may regret that you didn't even ask what KP meant, though."

"So, Nick," Derek said, pulling the attention back to the task at hand, "I'm going to have to reward your generous offer by making you fill out another stack of paperwork." Derek handed him the paperwork and consulted his clipboard. "OK, the designers have been wandering around, but they'll want the two girls to show them the bedrooms. The designers will take detailed photographs and measurements; then we'll all meet back here in a half hour."

"You think we'll be done with this paperwork by then?" Chickie's father asked the girls with a wink.

"I hope so," Chickie said, laughing. "We stars don't like to be kept waiting."

The girls met up with Petra and Claire at Chickie's house.

"I'm going to be working with Bree, doing your room, Chickie," Petra said.

"Great! I love your designs."

"I already know from the screen-test footage what

81

things you like and don't like, but as you know, we don't always do what you say you want."

"Why is that?" Briana asked.

"It's because good design stretches you. You can only visualize those things you've seen. We like to take it a step further and go for the new, the innovative—something we think you'll love, though you can't even have imagined it yet."

"Cool." Briana thought she'd like working with Petra.

"This room is definitely passé. Sort of a prepuberty pop-ad-art style." Petra smiled. "I'll bet you loved this room when you were little." Petra snapped digital images from every angle as she talked.

"Yep. I had many a princess fantasy in this room."

"OK. Help me do this measuring, and we'll head over to Bree's house."

Later as they walked over, Petra talked with Briana and Claire with Chickie. The teams were already getting to know each other.

"Answer one burning question that I haven't been able to find the answer to in any of the *Flip Flop* literature," Chickie asked as they got to Briana's house. "Why do the designers and Linley wear the same clothes two days in a row?"

Claire laughed. "We actually don't. We work so hard and the rooms are so tight, if we wore the same exact shirt—well, it doesn't take much imagination."

"We have at least two shirts that look exactly alike—maybe more," Petra said. "The reason is that the work is done in a haphazard fashion, not necessarily chronologically."

"That's right," Claire said. "The editors want the leeway to use some second-day scenes in the first half of the show if it makes the action flow better, and vice versa. By wearing the same shirt, we make that possible."

"OK, Bree, show us your room," Petra said.

Whatever. This was the awful part. Briana almost believed they could sense the trouble, the sadness, and the fear once they stepped inside her room. "This is my room. I call it the cave."

"Yes," Claire said, snapping images, "I recognize it from the footage. I agree with Linley—lovely proportions."

"I'll help you with the measuring," Petra said.

"We're going to have fun doing a design in here, Chickie," Claire said. "This house has lovely proportions—great bones, as we designers like to say." She took out her tape measure, handing one end to Linley. As the two moved around the room, she called out dimensions to Petra, who scribbled notations on the clipboard.

"OK, done for now," Petra said. "Let's get our marching orders from Derek and get back on the road. I'm anxious to start planning, aren't you, Claire?"

So far, so good. But there's no way this can keep going like this. Dad was bound to get involved, and then all the secrets would be laid bare.

Why did Briana feel such a sense of foreboding? Was it just her fears or something else—some sense of what might happen?

They headed back to the portable tables on the greenbelt.

Derek raised his clipboard. He was ready. "OK. There are still a million small details to take care of— that's right, we need to call Mosquito Abatement and make sure they spray the greenbelt before we get here.

It's summer and we often work late. We don't want to be eaten alive."

He paused and looked around. His eyes seemed to light on Briana. She felt tense enough without his scrutiny. She knew her dad would come unglued. *Why am I even pretending to be a normal American teenager? I'm so tired of lies.*

"A few last tips, girls. We want you to be yourselves, but we also want a little controversy and some drama."

Oh, you're likely to get drama. Why did Briana feel like crying? She began to breathe deeply, trying to fend off tears. As she looked up, she saw Petra watching her. The designer seemed to see right through Briana.

Briana recognized in Petra someone perceptive—someone who was used to seeing below the surface. *Just what I need when I'm trying to keep the messy underside from showing.*

There could be no retreat. The crazy roller-coaster ride continued up toward the stomach-dropping free fall. No turning back. No getting off. She had best just hang on for dear life.

God Grant Me Serenity

7

Bree, we're going to have firecrackers tonight. Wanna come?" Geoff bit off a piece of cinnamon roll.

"You're having firecrackers?" Briana squinted one eye. "Are you sure? Firecrackers are illegal."

"Geoff means sparklers. He calls them firecrackers." Sebastian poured orange juice into the glasses. "OK, I gotta know—was this your last sleepover in the pretty pink princess bedroom?"

Chickie grimaced. "I can't wait to get my redesign so I don't have to be tortured about my cutesy bedroom anymore."

Chickie and Briana continued setting the table for breakfast. Today was July fourth—a holiday from work for everyone—so breakfast was eat-it-whenever. Last night Mrs. Wells had made cinnamon rolls. It only took a couple of minutes in a warm oven, and they tasted like they'd just been baked.

Ever since deciding that they would be catering the *Flip Flop* meals, Chickie's parents had been testing all kinds of recipes. The Wells family and Briana eagerly performed the taste tests.

"Yum. These cinnamon rolls definitely make the cut," Sebastian said, taking a bite while sliding into his seat.

"Why, thank you." Mrs. Wells came into the kitchen. "Good. You set a place for Dad and me." She put another half-dozen rolls into the oven before sitting down. "Did you sleep well, Briana?"

"Yes. Thank you. I always sleep well here."

"We've been thinking about doing a trial run of the greenbelt canteen. No tent yet, but we want to see how the system will work."

"Sounds like the name of a restaurant—the Greenbelt Canteen." Chickie licked icing off a finger. "Or it could be a Mexican restaurant if you changed Canteen to Cantina."

"Channing—will you be serious." Her mom poked her in the side.

"Only if I have to." She smiled at her mom but sat straighter in her chair in mock seriousness.

"Anyway," Mrs. Wells continued, "we thought it might be fun to put together an impromptu Fourth of July block party on the greenbelt tonight. What do you think?"

"I get to do KP," Geoff called. When nobody fought him for the mysterious job, he asked, "What is KP?"

"It's a job you'll never forget, Bro," Sebastian said. Turning toward his mother, he said, "I think the party sounds like fun. Can I run into town and pick up more fireworks? I think we only have sparklers and a couple of Piccolo Petes left over from last year."

"Sure, but if we let everyone know, they'll bring their fireworks as well and we can pool them all."

"I'll do up some quick invitations on the computer," Chickie offered. "And Bree and I will deliver them to the families right around here."

"Your mom and dad will come, right, Briana?" Mrs. Wells took the cinnamon rolls out of the oven.

"My dad's not getting home till the weekend, but I'll see if Mom can come." Briana felt uncomfortable. Ever since the *Flip Flop* excitement, it had become harder and harder to keep her family cloistered. *The more people know about us, the more potential for trouble. When we stayed away and kept mysterious, no one looked at us too hard.*

"Earth to Bree. Earth to Bree." Chickie held her fist to her mouth as if it were a microphone.

"Where do you go when you leave us like that?" Sebastian asked. His smile took the sting out of his words.

Mrs. Wells had been scribbling on a tablet. "What do you guys think about food?"

"We like it," Geoff replied.

"As if I don't know that," his mother said with a laugh. "No, I mean do you think we should grill hamburgers or do something like teriyaki chicken?"

"Can we do both?" Chickie asked. "Some people don't do beef. Besides, hamburgers and chicken seem so American."

Briana didn't answer Sebastian's question. Not because she wanted to seem mysterious—although that was not half bad—she couldn't decide. She smiled instead. *A smile works.*

After she and Chickie finished designing and printing invitations, she let Chickie hand them out to the four families nearby while she went home to talk to Mom.

Why did she always approach Mom so cautiously? It's almost like they flinched, for fear they'd talk about "the elephant." Briana decided she loved that image—no wonder so many people used it. Living life with an alcoholic was just as outrageous.

Take her new uneasy, cautiously hopeful relationship with her mom. The elephant still dominated the living room, but instead of sitting on opposite sides of the pachyderm, it was like they decided to meet on the same side where they could at least see each other. It may not have reached June Cleaver standards, but it was better than polite avoidance.

Before she went into the kitchen to talk to her mom, she went upstairs and reached under the mattress. Pulling out the prayer, she read it over:

> God grant me the serenity
> To accept the things I cannot change;
> Courage to change the things I can;
> And wisdom to know the difference.

How the prayer had helped over the last couple of years. *Weird.* The thought came into her head that though the prayer had become a lifeline to God, she really didn't know God any better than she knew her mother. *I mean, I pray to Jesus to help me, but . . .*

She didn't really know what came after the "but." She had asked Jesus to help her keep a lid on things here. Had He? If she were honest, she'd have to say no. Things were spiraling out of control. *Out of control? Out of whose control? Where did that question come from? Have you talked to yourself so long that you are now asking yourself questions? OK, maybe I do like control. Could it be because I've lived in chaos for most of my life?*

She looked around her room. She saw books stacked neatly on the bookshelves from smallest to biggest. CDs arranged by artist and type of music. Shoes organized inside the closet by season. Three matching laundry baskets sat on the floor—whites, darks, gentle. *OK, so maybe order is important too.*

In the end, what does it matter? Things are happening, and there's no way to get out of them. Jesus, help! One more thought crossed her mind as she went downstairs to find Mom. *What if He is helping?*

"Mom?"

"I'm in here." She stood at the kitchen sink washing her hands. "I just finished making a cherry pie. It just seemed like a Fourth of July-ish thing to do."

"Did you plan to do anything tonight?"

"No. Oh, and your dad's not going to be home this weekend. Since he was in the Midwest this week and needs to be there next week, he decided it wasn't worth it to fly home in between. He said he'd just kick back at his hotel, watch TV, and use the pool."

"Do you miss him?" *Why did I ask that question?*

Her mom didn't answer at first. "I miss the old Fourth of July celebrations we used to have. Did you know that the first time your dad really noticed me was at an Independence Day picnic at Lake McClure? We had such fun in those days."

"I didn't know." Briana didn't really want to talk about it. Over the years her dad had become such a nonperson to her, she didn't know if she wanted to think of him any other way. Was he ever a person with hopes and dreams? Did he ever love her?

"You probably don't remember your dad before . . . I mean, before he was under such stress."

"No. I don't."

"Did you have plans for today?" her mom asked. She must have sensed that Briana wanted to change the subject.

"Actually, yes. Chickie's family decided to get together a sort of block party on the spur of the moment on the greenbelt. They asked some of the neighbors. They want us to come."

"Tonight?" Mom asked.

"I think they want to try out their catering ideas before the *Flip Flop* team descends on us."

"Is it a potluck?"

"Yes. Here's the invitation. They say to bring whatever we were going to cook, and we'll all share. Mr. Wells will barbecue."

"I guess we could bring cherry pie, and I have that big bag of sweet corn I got from a guy at work. If you pull back the cornhusks and pull out the corn silk, we can let Chickie's dad put them right on the barbecue—they'll steam in their husks."

"It sounds like you want to go."

"I liked Nick and Trish. It sounds casual and I think it would be fun."

Her answer surprised Briana.

"We can get those folding chairs off the hooks in the garage."

Her mom went out to the back porch and brought in the bag of corn. "Here, help me get the silk out. Be careful not to pull the husks off. After we do this, we'll soak them for an hour or so. Then the husks will have enough moisture to steam the corn."

They worked side by side, her mom giving her tips now and then. Mom showed her how to take a long husk that had fallen off and tear it into long strips to use to tie the husks back around the corn. When they were done, their corn "packages" looked interesting.

"I'll bet this is an idea Chickie's mom will use for the *Flip Flop* canteen. Doesn't it look cool?"

"It will taste even better." Her mom began scooping up all the corn silk to throw away. It stuck to everything. Before long, the two of them were laughing at the attempts to get every last one.

"We'll be finding strands of corn silk for days," Briana predicted. She couldn't believe she and her mom had spent an hour working side by side. "I'm going to call Chickie and tell her we're coming and let them know what we're bringing."

"Why don't you go into town to get a half gallon of vanilla ice cream for the pie and pick out a few rockets or sparklers for tonight?"

"I can do the ice cream, but you have to be eighteen to buy fireworks."

"That's right. It's been so long." Her mom got some money out of her wallet. "Do you think Chickie's brother would go along with you? I'd love to get the house straightened up before we go out to the party."

That was how Briana wound up in Sebastian's car going into town.

"This was a great idea, pooling our fireworks money," Sebastian said. "I think we should get a boxed assortment since they are the best value, but then we'll pick a few impressive fountains. Let's end with a Stars and Stripes—kind of a grand finale."

Chickie snorted from the backseat. "What is it about guys and fireworks?"

"Hey, don't knock it. We're lucky to live in the boonies where there's enough space that they still allow fireworks." Sebastian slowed down for a left turn. "Many places have outlawed fireworks."

"The little kids love it," Briana said, though she suspected that Sebastian and his friends might love it even more. "Don't forget to stop at the store for ice cream."

How nice it was to be with her friends, planning for a party that included her family. Sitting next to Sebastian made her feel happy and hopeful, but she was not ready to try to figure out why. If she were to be honest, she'd have a good idea.

Ever since the whole *Flip Flop* thing came up, her world had been opening up, one tiny crack at a time. She knew the risk of trouble increased with every chink that opened in the Harris family fortifications; but until things fell apart, she planned to enjoy the friendships, and she'd take pleasure in this tentative new thing with her mother.

✳　　　✳　　　✳

"What a great idea this was, Nick," said the neighbor who lived across the street. "Why don't we do this more often?"

Briana used tongs to take the steamed corn off one of the barbecues. She looked over at her mom talking to Chickie's mom. No doubt they were talking about the *Flip Flop* week. Chickie's mom and dad and her mom seemed as excited about it as she and Chickie were. In fact, it was at the top of everyone's mind at the picnic. One neighbor offered to help with the cooking, and all the women teased each other about Carpenter Chris.

Briana filled her plate and went to sit by her mom. Was this so cool? How she wished Michael and Matt could be here. Another one of the neighbors joined them.

"So, what is it your husband does?" the neighbor asked.

"He's marketing manager for an agricultural chemical firm."

Briana's stomach began to tighten. *Change the subject, Mom. Or get up and get more food. Or—*

"He's not home much, is he? We've only seen him a couple of times, pulling out of the driveway."

Mom shifted her food plate. "He's very successful at his career; but unfortunately, being national, his territory is huge."

Briana jumped up. "Mom, can I get you some more chicken? I think I'm going to have some more of that chili. It was delicious." Good thing she knew the neighbor brought that chili.

"Oh, you liked the chili? We've made it that way in my family for years. Lots of people don't think that chili con carne should have beans, but I find that . . ."

She was talking to Mom now, and it didn't look like she'd take a breath anytime soon. Briana waved goodbye as she took off, dropping off her plate on the way.

She went to the bench at the edge of the green—the one she and Chickie often used for hanging out. As she sat down, something in the pocket of her shorts poked her. She stood up and slid her hand into the pocket, pulling out the index card with her prayer printed on it. She'd forgot she put it in there.

She looked over at Mom fending off questions from neighbors. *Whatever made me pretend we could have a Beaver Cleaver day? If we're talking TV families, mine is probably more Osbornes than Cleavers. Well, not really, but there's no chance of us making a Hallmark Christmas commercial anytime soon. Isn't it amazing that no one has a clue about us?*

She looked at the card. "Accept those things I cannot change." *Is that the key? Acceptance? What does that mean?* She never tried to make believe her family was any different than it was. It's true she hid the truth from others, but she never hid the truth from herself. *Accept.* Could the fact that she tried so hard to control things mean that she didn't accept?

"You look so focused." Sebastian sat down next to her. She hadn't even seen him coming.

"Please tell me you're not studying," he said. "Especially in the middle of summer."

"I'm not studying," she said, holding the card against her side.

"OK," he teased. "What's the secret?"

"It's no secret."

"Just tell me it's not a letter from some love-struck high schooler." Sebastian batted his eyelashes, making Briana laugh.

"You'll be embarrassed when you see what it is." She handed the card to him. "It's a favorite prayer of mine."

"Boy, did you ever reel me in on that one," he said, laughing again as he took the card from her. "Oh, it's the 'Serenity Prayer.' Beautiful, isn't it?"

"It means a lot to me. I try so hard to take it to heart."

"What do you mean, 'take it to heart'?"

"I mean I keep trying to achieve the serenity of acceptance and the courage to change."

"How are you doing with your quest?" he asked.

"I don't know. Not so good, I guess, but reading the prayer often comforts me."

"You know why I asked?"

She didn't answer. *Is this a trick question?*

"I asked because I think you're missing the point." He put his hand over her hand. It was the first time he'd ever deliberately touched her, but it didn't seem like a boy-girl thing. The gesture took the sting out of his words.

"How am I missing the point?"

"Read me the first two words of the prayer."

"God grant."

"Right. There's the power in the prayer. It's not about trying to be accepting or trying to be courageous. You can just stop after the first two words."

"God grant?"

"Well, you don't really have to stop there—the prayer's beautiful—but when you've prayed the prayer, you asked God to grant you those things. You've done all you need to do."

"That's it?" Briana couldn't believe Sebastian really thought it was that easy.

"There's nothing more you need. I know it sounds sort of hokey, but it's something I'm working on—

something I'm learning—right now. We humans are so into trying and working and achieving and . . . well, you get the idea. God wants us to ask Him, to rely on Him, and to watch for His answer."

"What about the verse, 'God helps those who help themselves'?"

Sebastian laughed. "Dude, if you can find that one in the Bible, I'll give you another Cold Stone masterpiece with the works. And nuts."

"You mean that's not in the Bible?"

"Nope, though you could easily win a trivia contest with that one. Many people think it comes from the Bible."

"I didn't know you prayed." *That sounded terrible.* Briana rephrased it. "I mean, I know your family goes to church, and you can see it means a lot to your parents, but—"

"But you're wondering why I'm talking all churchy right now. You're probably remembering me when I was younger, right?"

Briana didn't answer.

Sebastian continued. "I went to church my whole life, but I didn't make my faith part of my life until college. I mean, I always believed it, but I just didn't let it affect the way I lived. Does that make sense?"

"I think so." She wasn't sure.

"It took a lot of searching and questioning until I was able to honestly say I didn't just want a Sunday kind of faith. I wanted my faith to be part of my whole existence—from sports to school to friendships—the whole enchilada."

"That's interesting."

He smiled and winked. "You're saying 'interesting.'

Are you sure you're not really thinking I'm off the deep end?"

"I'll never tell," she teased.

"Yikes!" he pointed over toward his house. "They're getting ready for fireworks. If I don't get over there, I may have to sit on the sidelines. Gotta run."

"Go." She waved him off. "And, Sebastian?"

He turned and raised an eyebrow at the question in her voice.

"Thank you. I'm going to think hard about what you said."

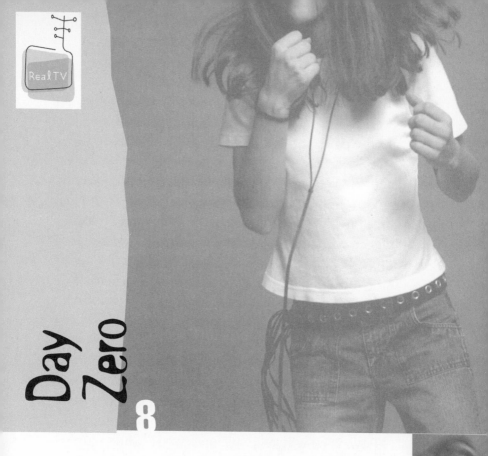

Day Zero

8

Get up, get up, get up!" Chickie sounded like a morning DJ, all chirpy and happy.

"Do you know what time it is? And do you know what time we finally stopped talking last night?" Briana pulled a pillow over her head as she groaned.

"Actually, we didn't stop talking until this morning, but who's counting?" Chickie practically vibrated with excitement. "You know what today is, don't you?"

"If I forget, I'm sure you'll be reminding me." Briana propped up on one elbow. "But who could forget? It's Day Zero of our wild and wonderful adventure."

"They'll be shooting footage in about three hours. It doesn't give us much time to get ready." Chickie headed toward the bathroom. "I'll shower while you try to wake up."

"Chickie Wells, before you go, if I forget to tell you . . . well, thank you for all this."

"Are you really down with this? Sometimes I feel as if I dragged you kicking and screaming into this whole adventure."

"All I know is that I'm so excited today, I'm actually ready to jump out of bed." Briana meant what she said. Who knew what would happen, but she decided she would enjoy every minute—somehow.

"I'm jumping in the shower. The worst thing about the show is that in twenty-four hours I have to say good-bye to you and I won't get to see you again until all this is over."

"I know. Who will keep me energized?" She sat up and hugged her knees. "Go. Take your shower or we are going to run out of time."

As Chickie disappeared into the bathroom, Briana thought about the next three days. She meant what she said about enjoying the experience. She planned to work as hard at living in the moment as she would work at creating a gorgeous room for Chickie.

Worry often crept in—no question. In fact, she'd only been awake ten minutes and she was wondering what went on last night at their house. Dad was between trips but would leave this afternoon to drive to Las Vegas for a series of meetings. That would put him home for part of today, but he'd be gone by the time

Chickie and Claire were scheduled to take over the Harris house.

They called today Day Zero—the day they would film the footage for the B-roll. Everyone not involved in that project would be setting up Camp Carpentry and the sewing center. All preparations had to be finished by tonight.

As the trucks pulled in last night, Chickie and Briana figured fully half the town showed up. What fun. Briana wasn't used to being the center of a whirlwind—well, at least not this kind of exciting whirlwind.

"Your turn. Don't forget to deep-condition your hair."

"Yes, ma'am."

"As soon as you get out, we need to talk." Chickie loosened the thick towel wrapped around her hair.

"Who's up? Do I need to put on a robe before going in, or can I make a run for it in my jammies?"

"If you're asking about Sebastian, he left early this morning to begin work on the carpentry area of the greenbelt."

"I wasn't worried about Geoff, that's for sure."

"Hurry."

After her shower, Briana flopped on the bed once more. "You said you wanted to talk. I'm all ears."

"First of all, remember way back when we were watching that Texas show with Petra and Claire?"

"I remember. The one where one of the girls asked for romantic and pastel and ended up with fire-engine red?"

"Yeah. That's the one." Chickie smeared a greenish lumpy cream on her face. "I remember you saying, 'I pity the poor girl who gets Petra.'"

"I said that, huh?"

"Yep. Those very words." Chickie sighed. "I like Petra's designs—it's such fun to watch them unfold because they can be so outrageous. But when it comes to the room you have to live in day in and day out, it's a little more scary." Chickie looked into the mirror, poking at the lumpier spots of cream on her face. "When they first assigned Petra to work with you, I felt relieved. It wasn't until a couple of days ago that it dawned on me—if she's working with you, it means she's designing *my* room. Duh!"

"Right. It gets very confusing, doesn't it? You're working with Claire, but you guys are doing my room."

Chickie stretched out on the floor, goopy face and all. "So how can we protect each other?"

"I have no idea." Briana had seen guests tell their friends what they would hate, and somehow they ended up with something close to their worst nightmare. The funny thing is that they usually ended up loving it. "What would you hate?"

"I thought a lot about this—maybe too much. I would hate anything that resembles my current room. No pink, no white furniture."

"I knew that."

"I also don't want anything overly themed. I know you won't be able to control this element at all, since it's a design thing, but I'd hate to have a room that has a name."

"I don't get it—a name?"

"Yeah, like when we talk about the Out-of-Africa bedroom or the Ride-to-the-Hounds-Hunt-Club room. It seems contrived."

"I know. In trying to make their rooms memorable, sometimes the designers go way over the top."

Chickie got up and leaned into the small mirror above her dresser as she tissued off the facial mask. "What I want is like you have in your room—a system. I'd like to have a place designed for everything."

"Leave that to me. I'm *so* there."

"How about you?"

"You know the lightness I crave. I already have organizational systems. I'd like even better systems, but I'd be very disappointed if I ended up with a catchall kind of feel to the room. Nothing casual, nothing messy. Keep reminding Claire that I'm into precise, controlled, neat."

"Yeah, they'll probably do a psychedelic bedroom for you with a bead curtain covering your closet and big messy pillows all over the floor."

"Yuck; can't you just see it?" Briana pulled her clothes on. They'd spent days deciding what to wear for every waking minute. Briana was glad they put the time into it. Thanks to Chickie, there would be no fashion angst.

"Back to my original question. What about Petra?" Chickie asked.

"Actually, the more I studied the rooms she did, the more I'm drawn to her design signature. I think she and I can do a room for you that rocks."

"I'm so glad to hear it. I mean, I know the experience is enough, but we've been thinking about this for so long. I probably have unrealistic hopes, but it won't be the first time."

"And maybe we'll get rooms that are way better than we imagined," Briana said.

"I just can't believe the time has finally come."

"I need to run home and pack my bag. I also want to

make sure my room is decent enough for America to see." Briana gathered up her things and stuffed them in her bag. "I know you'll be loading my room out first thing on the show, but can you imagine how humiliating it would be to move the bed and find a dirty sock or something?"

"We're going to go out to the dairy to watch them film the B-roll, right?" Chickie asked, changing the subject.

Derek and Linley had finally settled on a state-of-the-art Jersey dairy out in the country not too far from town to use for the opening footage. The dairy featured a new carousel milking parlor. Derek figured he could get some great shots of the designers, Linley, and Carpenter Chris hamming it up around the cows.

"I wouldn't miss it," Briana said. Now that they were committed to the experience, she planned to enjoy it. "I think the whole town will be out there."

"We've got less than an hour now."

"OK, I'm out of here. Can you pick me up at my house? Just honk and I'll come." Briana headed toward home. She walked across the green, waving to Sebastian and another guy erecting the canopy over the area that would house *Flip Flop*'s famous Camp Carpentry.

When they had come for their planning session, Derek couldn't stop talking about the greenbelt. Too often, they had to set up Camp Carpentry in the driveway of someone's home.

As Briana walked into the house, she saw her mom and dad sitting at the kitchen table. *When was the last time that happened during the day?*

"Good morning," her dad said to her. "Want to come have a bite of breakfast?"

Her dad was eating breakfast? "Sure. Whatever."

Mom seemed so happy. "Dad wants to go with us out to the dairy to watch the filming."

No. What is she saying? What if he gets upset? What if—

"I can't get out of the Las Vegas trip, but I'd hate to miss all the fun. It's not every day your daughter debuts on national television." He took another bite of pancakes.

"Can I make you a couple pancakes, honey?" Mom asked her.

"Sure. Whatever." *Did I take a wrong turn and walk into a different house?*

"You sound tired. Did you girls stay up most of the night to talk?" Her mom's words sounded light, but Briana could see that more than anything, her mom wanted Briana to join with her in happiness.

"We did." *There. A reason.* "In just a few hours it'll all begin. I guess I'm a little nervous." *Several reasons.*

Her mom smiled.

This is too weird. I mean, I'm happy that Dad is sober and even trying to be part of our lives, but I can't remember the last time . . . and Mom is playing along like this is normal?

"Here you go." Mom put the golden-brown pancakes in front of her.

Briana thought of her prayer, up in her room, under the mattress. *God grant me the serenity to accept the things I cannot change. Maybe I need to treat this the same way I decided to handle the* Flip Flop *experience—enjoy the moment and savor the memories.*

"These pancakes are great, Mom."

"I agree. Anna, you are still the best cook," Dad said.

Mom put her hand on his shoulder and he covered it with his hand.

I need to savor this moment, but will it make it hurt all the more when it all comes crashing down? She felt as if they'd gone a step further. The elephant may still be in the living room, but instead of ignoring it, they were trying to get the elephant to sit on a settee and take tea. *I'm definitely losing it,* Briana thought. She couldn't help smiling at the picture.

"We're going to head out to the dairy about ten. Do you want to ride with us?" her mom asked.

"No. I'll let you two have some time. Chickie and I are going together. We can't believe that pretty soon we'll have to separate."

"I'll bet you never did something this big without Chickie by your side before." Mom understood.

"We'll see you there."

She'd hardly washed the syrup off her hands when Chickie showed up to pick her up. Two quick toots of the horn and Briana headed out the door. "Bye. I'll see you there."

Once in the car, Briana looked at her friend and said, "There's no turning back now. Our *Flip Flop* has begun."

"I know. I keep thinking of things I want to impress on you before we start."

"What? Like don't put your elbows on the table?"

"No. Like remembering I hate aqua. And if they do something with lava lamps, I'm moving out. And no organic things, like grass growing on my headboard. And—"

"Like I'm going to have any say in this." Briana thought about the whole process. "Whatever happens, we need to just decide to go with the flow, laugh a lot, and enjoy every minute."

"You are right. OK, if they put grass on my headboard, you have my permission to consider it a huge joke."

"Face it; we have no input. They may ask us what we want, but in the end it will be what it will be."

"That's how we have to take it because we have no control. If we try to control something that's outside our control, we'll miss out on the experience."

Duh. Like I haven't been living that in my own life. Briana often wondered if she shouldn't have confided some of her secrets to Chickie. After all, if nothing else, her friend had proven herself loyal and trustworthy. *It's not like I worry that if she knew, she'd be any different.* Oh, well, enough of that. Her job these next three days was to have fun.

"Earth to Bree. Earth to Bree. Are you thinking of herbaceous nightmares in your room?"

"I don't even want to go there. I think my worst nightmare would be to find some hokey mural on my wall or to have the room themed around some funny idea. Remember the Monkeys-in-Paradise room?"

"Oh, thanks for the visual. How did I forget that one?" Chickie turned onto the road leading out to the dairy. "Let's make a pact."

"OK."

"We'll have fun and not stress about the design choices."

"Right. And if either of our rooms turns out nightmarish, we'll pool our money afterward and do our own *Flip Flop.*"

"Deal."

"One more thing," Briana said as Chickie pulled into the drive for the dairy. "We need to remember every single off-camera detail so we can totally catch up with each other when this is all over."

"How are we gonna stand this? To be going through this whole thing and not be able to talk to each other? I may not make it."

"I know. A slumber party without you? Too strange."

Chickie pulled up to the area where dozens of cars were already parked. They saw the *Flip Flop* truck, back doors open.

"Looks like the place," Chickie said. "My parents are here already."

"This is the biggest thing to ever hit Mercey Springs. Does it ever hit you that you are the reason all this is happening?"

"As long as everyone doesn't blame me if things go wrong."

They walked toward the milking parlor. The Johnson Dairy had only been finished for about a year, and it was the pride of Mercey Springs. A wide expanse of lawn greeted visitors. The dairy had been designed for minimum environmental impact and maximum efficiency. The *Flip Flop* team planned to highlight the 100 percent recyclable factor.

Linley stood by the stacks of feed talking into the camera as Chris, Petra, and Claire sat on a rail fence. The show always tried to have an understated educational element to their B-roll.

"Cut." Derek turned to the cameraman. "I think our best shots would be inside the carousel thing, or whatever those computer things are. We can get those pretty cow faces looking down on our team."

Briana laughed. "So much for technical terms." The

cows were milked on what looked like a huge merry-go-round. It was such fun to watch.

Everyone went into the milking parlor. The visitors stood off to one side as the cameramen got set up for a few shots of the carousel.

Briana saw her mom and dad come in. It seemed so strange to see them out together. Her stomach tightened. She couldn't help it—she always waited for the incident that would set off the chaos. It never failed to come.

"Linley, would you grab that bucket and do the washing part for just a minute?" Derek motioned toward a worker washing off the cow's udders before putting the equipment from the milking machine on.

Linley stood near the van. She was doing a touch-up of her makeup.

"Yeah, baby," Briana said with a huge laugh. "She's really gonna be down with that."

Chickie laughed. "Look at our parents. How cool is that?" All four were standing and talking together.

"Cool," Briana said, meaning exactly the opposite. She watched her father's every twitch. She'd learned to read his body language. *OK, he looks relaxed enough. Jesus, help him feel comfortable. Don't let him find any reason to need a drink.* Especially since he had to drive to Las Vegas this afternoon. As much as she hated her father's drinking and the upheaval that followed, she worried about him all the time. Much of his drinking happened other places, meaning he drove the car while drunk. Briana had seen way too many Mothers Against Drunk Driving videos at school. She could barely watch, thinking it could be her dad. More and more lately, he'd have a cab drive him home. That much was a good change.

"You want me to do what?" Linley burst out into peals of laughter. "Oh, I'm so glad I touched up my makeup."

"She's a good sport, isn't she?" Chickie whispered.

The cows stood in a long line, waiting to step onto a stall on the carousel as it turned slowly.

"I wonder what makes them want to get on there?" Chickie asked.

Mr. Johnson, the dairyman, stood behind her. "Just look at the heaviness of their udders. They are anxious to have that pressure relieved."

"Oh, hi, Mr. Johnson," said Briana. He went to their church.

"Are you girls excited about this?"

"Excited, scared, nervous—all rolled into one," Chickie said.

"Is that your father over there, Briana? I've never met him. What do you say I go over and invite him to church?" He winked at Briana.

Well, if he wasn't uncomfortable before . . . Briana watched closely as Mr. Johnson introduced himself. Her dad smiled and put out his hand. *I wonder if this is how he is at work? He seems so happy. If only he could be this way in real life. I'd be so proud of him.* Mom stood by, beaming. Hopeful. Was there hope?

Linley walked over to the worker standing on the ground below the carousel platform. She couldn't keep her face from wrinkling in disgust. "I don't think my contract covers this, Derek." She watched as the man carefully washed the cow's udder using a hose of warm water and a glove. "Will there be time for a fresh manicure?"

"This will be so funny; I hope they use this footage," Chickie said as Linley slipped on the gloves and took the hose and began washing the udders as the cows slowly rotated. "She's not bad at this."

"OK," Derek directed, "the rest of you get in there. Petra and Claire, why don't you sit on that platform right behind? Chris, you sit on the steps. All of you give advice."

The three of them took their places. Claire wiped off the platform carefully before sitting down, causing everyone to laugh. Then the catcalls began. Chris took out his watch and hassled Linley about the time—mimicking her worried routine on the show.

Laughter punctuated every comment. The segment showed off the personalities.

Briana looked over at her parents. Dad laughed along with everyone else. A couple of times he leaned over to make a comment to either Mr. Johnson or Chickie's dad. Weird. It was definitely a *Leave It to Beaver* moment.

"OK, and . . . cut." Derek smiled. "We got some great footage. You're a good egg, Linley."

"Oh, don't think you're not going to pay for this, Derek Samuelson," Linley said with a laugh.

"Let's go down into the pit, or whatever they call that." He referred to the underground room that housed all the carousel controls.

Chickie and Briana followed the crowd down the cool cement stairs into a large room below. It was open to the carousel above, so as you looked up you saw cow faces looking down on you, slowly circling around. Tubes and controls ran every which way.

"Each cow's milk is measured by these individual

computers," Mr. Johnson said to Chickie's and Briana's dads. "We track their output and test the milk here."

Dad is enjoying himself with these guys. She watched him closely. No sign of discomfort. No antsy movements yet.

"Hmmm. I don't see how we can really involve the team with the cows because of the distance between the cow faces and our faces." Derek turned to one of the cameramen. "If I set Petra and Claire up here with their design pads, do you think you could get an angle that includes their head shots, the pads, the computer thingies with milk going through, and those pretty cow faces?"

The cameramen started angling and changing tripod heights. The cows continued to chew their cuds, but they watched every movement with interest.

"My Jersey girls are enjoying the show as much as we are," said Mr. Johnson.

As the filming wrapped up and the crew packed up, Briana watched her mom and dad say their good-byes to Chickie's parents and to Mr. Johnson.

Things will never be the same. The thought made Briana's mouth go dry. With isolation came safety, but now that her dad had met everyone, how could they ever keep to themselves again? *How will I feel when the truth comes out?*

"I'm going to have to take off for my meeting, honey." Dad gave her a kiss on the cheek. How long had it been since that had happened? "Have a good time and enjoy the whole experience so you can tell me about it when I get home."

When had she ever been able to tell him about her life? "Yeah, sure."

Her mom looked straight at her, though her expression told Briana nothing.

She thought of her prayer. Wisdom to know the difference between what can be changed and what can't. She didn't have a clue if anything could be changed. If Sebastian were here, he'd probably remind her that God did. *Jesus, help me.* She looked at her dad, walking toward the car. "Bye, Dad. Safe trip."

He turned back toward her with a smile and a wave. He turned and put his arm around Mom.

"That B-roll will rock," Chickie said. "What fun!"

Yeah. What fun. Briana wished her life were less complicated, but she had to admit, this morning was like no morning she could remember. *OK, it was fun. Sort of.*

Derek Samuelson gathered everyone around the van, outside the dairy. "Good job. I think it'll be a great B-roll." He laughed. "Good thing we got Monterey with the whole Cannery Row footage and L.A. with Rodeo Drive filming between the rodeo and the dairy footage. We don't want our stars looking like hicks."

"Hey, I resemble that," Mr. Johnson said with mock umbrage.

Derek just laughed. "OK, here's what comes next." He flipped some pages on his clipboard before his assistant brought a new clipboard and took the old one. "That's better."

"Eighteen hours until we have to say good-bye to each other," Chickie whispered, grabbing Briana's hand.

"Petra and Claire, you're finishing up your shopping and plans, right? Make sure you let Chris and Joe know how much wood you need for projects."

"Who's Joe?" Briana whispered.

"He's the real craftsman. remember? Linley told us Carpenter Chris is mostly window dressing."

Briana laughed, covering her mouth to keep the sound from interrupting. Chickie could be so blunt. She wondered what the ever-so-beautiful Chris would think about being dismissed so lightly.

"I want all the techs to work on getting the overhead cameras set up in each room and checking all the equipment to make sure it's working. Did we replace that one lapel mic that kept giving us a buzz last week?"

"I'll check," the older cameraman said.

"Trish and Nick," Derek said after checking his clipboard, "you set up the canteen. Sebastian and Joe have Camp Carpentry set up already, and by the time you get back they should have the tent and the makeshift dining room all set up." He looked up from his clipboard. "Man, we've never had it so good with this greenbelt. We may get spoiled."

"That's OK," Mr. Wells said. "Our ninety-five-plus summer temperatures will temper your enthusiasm. We plan to have cases and cases of chilled water on hand. If time allows, we'll have homemade ice cream at the hottest part of the day, say, four."

"Sounds good." Derek continued, "Suzanne's already in the sewing center getting everything set up.

Both designers have already given her some specs, so she's ready to start on the projects this afternoon. Anna should be there now as well."

"Briana and Channing, you look puzzled." Derek smiled. "I guess it's time to give you more behind-the-scenes skinny."

The *Flip Flop* team laughed.

"Our job is to create a fast-paced, exciting show for our viewers. You two will be the stars of the show, but as you know, you will not have to do every little thing with your own hands."

Chickie pretended to wipe sweat off her brow.

"We make it seem like it's just the teens, the designers, Carpenter Chris, and Linley because it's so much more fun to have a limited cast of characters. But there's no way you could pull off the complicated redos we do in forty-eight hours with only two people and half of two helpers."

"What we do," Linley broke in, "is create magic for the camera. It's not to say we don't work like crazy. We may film you doing a couple seams on a pillow, but if you think we've got time to do velvet corded pillows along with everything else . . ."

"Linley's right," Derek said. "We all work hard to make it happen. There's been many a show where I had to get down and lay flooring to keep things moving."

"It's not dishonest to imply that both rooms are complete with only six people, is it?" Chickie's dad asked.

"No," Derek said. "We never state that categorically. We make it seem like that for the weekly show, but fans who want to dig deeper tend to visit our Web site, where we give the whole picture."

"That's right," Linley said. "Serious *Flip Flop* fans know everything about us. In fact, you know Joe's never appeared on camera, but he has a whole Internet fan site." She laughed. "Prepare to become famous, girls. You have no idea how dedicated our fans are."

"Before you get the wrong idea," Derek said, putting his hands up, "the budget is nonnegotiable—there is no wiggle room. Same with the time crunch. When Linley asks for an accounting, it must be to the penny, and if she looks at her watch—believe it."

Linley nodded with her best hard-nosed school-marm expression.

"OK," Derek said. "Let's head back. I think I covered everything."

Everyone started toward the cars. "Oh, one question." Derek looked at Chickie's dad. "What's for lunch?"

Everyone laughed.

"Grilled hamburgers—cheese optional. Salads for the diet-conscious."

"As if." Briana loved Mr. Wells's hamburgers.

The girls ended up flitting from place to place. It was all too exciting. All day long, cars would drive by, slowing down to watch. Several kids from school came by and stopped to ask if the girls could get autographs for them.

Chris saw the crowds and came over to sign autographs, making the crowds even bigger.

Briana could see who would do the real work. Joe and Sebastian worked the entire time Chris autographed and posed for photos. Derek finally came by and encouraged Chris to wind it up.

Briana wished she could hang out in Camp Carpentry. It would be such fun to watch Sebastian working like a real pro, but since at the moment the carpenters were doing jobs for both rooms, Briana and Chickie couldn't peek.

They helped Chickie's parents clean up after lunch and start the preparations for dinner.

"Can you believe this is really happening?" Briana asked. "I keep thinking I'll wake up and find out I dreamt this whole thing."

"I know. I can't believe I had the guts to apply."

"And that we were picked!"

"It has to be a God thing. I'd love to figure out why God wanted us to have this in our lives. I mean, doesn't it seem like He usually brings things into our lives that make us grow or that challenge us? I keep trying to figure out the growing edge."

I don't need to figure it out. I wonder if Chickie's right. Could God be using Flip Flop *to do something in my messed-up family? Or is it for me?*

"Or maybe God's just like our parents sometimes," Chickie continued. "He just likes to do fun things for us because He loves us."

"Whatever the why part, I'm just going to try to enjoy every minute," Briana said.

Linley came by. "Bree, if you want to go get familiar with the sewing center, now would be a good time, since they are working on something for Chickie's room."

Chickie widened her eyes and gave Briana a nudge with her elbow and a broad wink.

"Oh, yeah," Linley said. "You need to take the pledge. Hold up your right hands."

Both girls straightened up and raised their hands.

"Repeat after me. I promise not to reveal a single detail of my friend's *Flip Flop* . . ."

The girls repeated the phrase.

". . . Or Linley Prior will reveal the contents of my diary on national television."

Briana blanched. "You don't have my diary, do you?"

Linley laughed. "No, silly. I'm just trying to impress on you that we do have to keep things totally under wraps. We can't get dramatic reveal footage if any of the details have leaked out during the makeover. It ruins the climax."

Briana knew she looked relieved. "OK. I promise, if you promise never to even joke about diaries again."

"Channing—I mean, Chickie—you can go check out Camp Carpentry to get a feel for how things work there. At four o'clock, projects will be switched, and you two can switch centers. Then we'll meet to go over everything at five thirty in the canteen. Dinner's at six."

Briana walked over to her garage.

"Hi, Briana," Mom said, and turning to the thirty-something woman working on the other sewing machine, she introduced them. "Suzanne, this is my daughter, Briana. Briana, Suzanne Maher. She's the genius responsible for all the gorgeous linens and upholstery on *Flip Flop*."

"Nice to meet you, Suzanne," Briana said. "Derek said we were all on a first-name basis, right?"

"Right. After working together madly for three days, you'll see that we'll know each other way too close to be formal."

"You're not supposed to really see the color theme until the paint reveal, but what do you think so far?" Suzanne held up several squares of fabric with a foreign

120

feel to them. They ranged from coffee colors to terra cotta to reds—many of them threaded with gold.

"Oh, I feel a theme coming on—I hope it won't rival Monkeys in Paradise," Briana said.

Suzanne wrinkled her nose. "Oh, you do watch the show. Don't feel bad; you only had to *watch* that episode. I spent three days of my life sewing monkeys."

Briana laughed.

"No; Petra may be known for outrageous designs, but in reality she loves beautiful fabrics, and her rooms are easy to live in—classic, actually."

"Hmmmm. So if that's Petra's style, what can I expect from Claire?"

"Good try, but my lips are sealed." She went back to her machine. "I have noticed, though, that Claire is our people pleaser. She may be less over the top because she bends over backward to give the teens their dream bedrooms."

"Oh, I so hope so." Briana remembered that she went on and on during their screen test about her perfect design—it was all on tape. She wondered if Claire had watched the footage.

"I'm heading out for a cold drink and a scoop of that homemade ice cream. Anyone want to come?" Suzanne asked.

"No; I've just gotten going, though I wouldn't object if you brought back of a cup of ice cream for me." Briana's mom smiled from behind her sewing machine.

"OK. Bree?"

"No, thanks. I'll be going that way later."

Once Suzanne left, Mom started sewing again.

"Wasn't it wonderful to see the old Brian—Dad—today?" Her voice held a note of wistfulness.

Briana didn't know how to respond. She decided honesty usually worked best. "I don't know, Mom. I never remember seeing that side of him."

"You don't remember when you were in primary school, before his job became such a pressure cooker?"

"I don't think so."

"The way he was today is the way I always think of your dad. The drinking part seems so recent and so out of character."

Briana didn't say anything. How could two people in the same house see things so differently?

"We moved to Mercey Springs because we hoped the more laid-back pace would allow your dad to escape some of the tension and go back to his old self," Mom said.

"But this is where all my memories are, and all I can think about are the horrible nights that go on forever," Briana said.

"I know. When everything gets too much for your father, he blows." Mom continued to sew as she talked. "Even when he's been drinking, though, he's never laid a hand on you kids or me, no matter how upset he's been."

"And that's good, Mom? The things he's said to us have been . . . have been . . ."

"I know it's been ugly, but you know that's not him."

"I do?" Briana couldn't believe her mom felt this was a sort of temporary craziness. "Mom, why do you think Matt and Michael escaped?"

"I know. I know, but . . ."

Briana could see her Mom retreating again. Why ruin the fun of this time with a rehash of all this mess?

"Let's just not think about this now, OK? I want to just have fun and enjoy the *Flip Flop* experience."

"Me too. I just felt hopeful after seeing the old Brian." Mom turned the corner on the pillow top she was sewing. "I think we need to really talk, Briana. You know, I wrote to your brothers and got letters back from them."

"I didn't know that."

"I wish I knew what I could do to make everything better."

"But, Mom, what if you can't make it better? I've been thinking that I need to find a way to make things good even if everything isn't fixed." Briana sat down next to her. "That's why I wrote to Matt and Michael."

"I wondered what made you reach out."

"I figured that even if our family was falling apart—"

"We're not falling apart, Briana. This is a setback—a problem, that's for sure, but we're not falling apart."

"Whatever." Briana started to pull back again but decided not to lose the candor of the moment because of word choice. "Maybe we are not falling apart, but I decided that we couldn't let Dad's problem keep us separated from each other."

"I'm impressed. I mean, I tend to pull in and shut my eyes to the problem. Your decision was a much better one than mine."

"You know what helped me the most, Mom?"

"What?"

"I found a prayer called the 'Serenity Prayer.'"

"I know it," Mom said, lifting up the presser foot on the sewing machine.

"It helped me because it talks about two categories of things—those that can be changed and those that can't. I've been trying to divide things up under those headings and stop spending so much of my life wishing I could change things over which I have no control."

"Hmm." Mom stopped sewing. "I've never really seen it that black-and-white."

Briana laughed. "I'm a sort of black-and-white concrete thinker according to my English teacher."

"So that's why you took me out to lunch and contacted your brothers? Because that was something you could change?"

"Yes. It made me feel so good to be able to change something in my life."

"And your dad is something you cannot change, right?"

"I can't change, I can't predict—Mom, I can't even get out of going downstairs to listen to him rant and rave or else cry and apologize hour after hour."

Her mother didn't say anything.

"I don't mean to hurt you, Mom, by saying those things."

"I know you don't. I guess I just haven't seen it through your eyes or your brothers' eyes. I've seen it as a temporary thing that your dad needs to get out of his system."

Now it was Briana's turn to hold her tongue.

"You probably think I'm in denial."

"Oh, Mom, I don't know what I think. I'm only trying to think about the things I can do something about."

"That definitely makes sense. This whole *Flip Flop* thing has sure turned us upside down."

Briana laughed. "Good, Mom. *Flip Flop?* Upside down? Cute play on words."

"Unintentional, of course. Don't you be expecting your aged mom to be witty."

"But I know what you're saying. When Chickie first mentioned she was going to apply, I nearly died. You do know that no one—not even Chickie—knows about Dad's drinking."

"I figured that out while getting to know Nick and Trish. They think the reason we've kept to ourselves is my shyness and your dad's travel schedule."

"At first I made myself practically sick worrying about all of our secrets coming out, but I finally decided there's nothing I can do about it. I mean, I'm still petrified when I think of how I'd feel if Dad came into our house drunk when a whole houseful of people were there." Briana groaned at the thought. "With this trip to Las Vegas, though, we avoided that. I'm so grateful."

Mom was quiet for the longest time. "Your dad did say he hated missing all the fun and that if there was any way he could get out of the last set of meetings, he'd try to be home tomorrow night or for the reveal at the latest."

"No, Mom." Briana had trouble catching her breath. "Please, Mom, figure a way to talk him out of it, please."

"What are you trying to wheedle out of your hard-working mother, Bree?" Suzanne said as she walked in the door. Neither one of them heard her coming. "Here's your ice cream, Anna. It's fresh peach and is it ever to die for."

"Thank you." Her mom scooted her chair back from the machine and took a bite.

"Bree, they need you over at Camp Carpentry, and we need Channing—I mean, Chickie—over here. Get some ice cream on your way." She turned to Mom. "We need to put away all this fabric before Chickie gets here and take out the other projects. That's how it works:

You just get one thing going and you have to worry about another."

Yep. Briana couldn't help dwelling on the possibility of her dad coming home early. *You just get one thing worked out and you have to worry about another.*

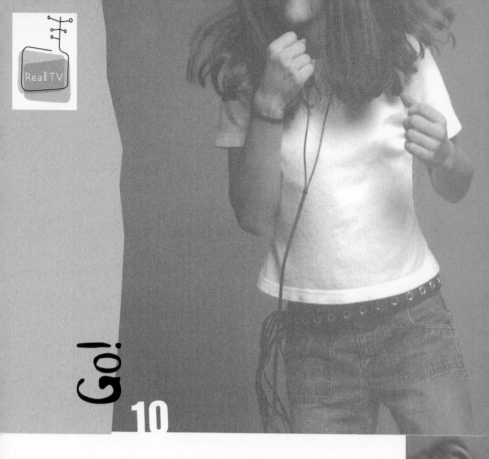

The smell of garlic made concentration difficult as everyone gathered in the canteen for Derek's five-thirty meeting. Chickie's parents were doing Caesar salads; plates of fresh mozzarella sliced with homegrown tomatoes and pesto were already out on the tables. Spaghetti sauce had been simmering since lunch. Briana guessed that Chickie's mom was in the house boiling the pasta and getting garlic bread ready to go. Who could think about details?

"OK, team, stop eyeing the food," Derek

said. "It was hot with a capital *H* today. I figured that since we have sunlight until after nine o'clock tonight, we should eat dinner; and then let's go ahead and film the key swap tonight. Is that OK with everyone?"

One of the cameramen spoke up. "We should be able to put the girls in a place where we can't see long shadows behind them. I think it will work fine."

"We can look at it afterward—before tomorrow morning—to make sure it worked, but it will save us time tomorrow and let us get right into the work."

The assistant handed him a new clipboard. "OK. Intro to the designers at nine. Petra's paint reveal will be at nine-thirty; Claire's at ten." He flipped the page and then flipped back. "Oh, that's right—do you girls have your bags packed? You'll need them as props for the key swap."

Both girls nodded their heads.

"Good. Now, let's see. Designers? You are going into town with us to stay at the hotel tonight, right?"

"Yes," Petra said. "I think we're set here."

"OK. If you girls plan to bunk together again tonight"—he looked at Chickie and Briana—"I'd prefer you do it over there." He pointed to Chickie's house. "It might be too great a temptation to sneak down into the sewing center and poke around a bit."

The girls looked at each other, trying for a look of injury, but they ended up bursting into giggles instead.

"See, that's what I figured," Derek said over their protests. "Parents can sleep at their own houses, of course."

He looked at his assistant. "Have I left anything out?"

His assistant took the clipboard and flipped the pages. "I don't think so."

"OK, team members know this; but to make a show great, we need you all to sparkle. Keep thinking sparkle." He twisted his fingers in his cheeks as if to deepen dimples. "Our job is to make you unforgettable—to coax your personalities out."

Linley piped in, "Be sure to get enough sleep tonight. When we have problems with dull guests, it's usually a sleep issue. We'll do our best to pull you out, but you need to do your part by staying engaged and excited."

"You need to forget the cameras," Derek added. "If you can forget them, our viewers will forget them. Especially during the slumber party segments. We want those to look intimate and personal."

"That's not an easy trick when you have a cameraman there as well," Linley said.

"OK. Any questions?" Derek asked.

"When's dinner?" Chris asked with a grin.

"Looks like now," Sebastian said as he saw his mom bringing a huge basket of garlic bread and his dad the pot of spaghetti noodles.

Chickie's dad put the pot down and turned to Derek. "Would it be OK if I asked a blessing on the food?"

"Sure," Derek answered.

"As we gather with friends old and new, we come into Your presence, Lord Jesus. Bless those gathered and bless the food we are about to eat. In Jesus' name we pray. Amen."

A few murmured "amen," and the line began to form for dinner.

"Can I sit with you girls?" Sebastian asked.

"Sure," said Chickie. "Especially if we can wheedle some details out of you. You've been working hard all day, so we know you must already have plans you're working from."

"My lips are sealed," he said, pressing his lips tightly together.

"Hey, why not?" Briana said. "Sealed lips mean there's more for us to eat."

"OK, they're sealed with a one-way valve. Things can go in but nothing can come out."

"That's too much information for me," Chickie said.

"Can I join you?" Joe, the master carpenter, came up with a plate of food.

"Sure." Sebastian scooted his chair over closer to Briana to make room, but Joe took his chair and moved it over by Chickie.

Sebastian made all the introductions, though they'd met briefly before.

"You don't know how happy I am to be eating home-cooked food." Joe sighed and closed his eyes. "The smell alone is almost enough."

"I take it you usually don't have home-cooked food," Briana said.

"They usually get caterers, but they use a lot of pre-pared foods, and because the schedules are often tight, it's just not possible to do much more than sandwiches. Other times we go to restaurants."

"It sounds so romantic," Chickie said, "but I'll bet it gets old after a while."

"Mostly it's fun. I love working with wood—not that we can often afford good woods, but to be able to do what I love and meet so many interesting people . . ."

"I hear you have your own fan site," Briana said.

"Is that weird or what?" Joe seemed like a totally nice, non-stuck-up guy.

They talked and laughed throughout the meal, finding out about Joe's family and talking about the show. Joe had just got up to get dessert when Derek stood up at another table.

"I understand Trish baked German chocolate cake for dessert, but before you all jump up, here's the plan. We'll hold off on dessert; Linley and the girls will brush their teeth, put on their *Flip Flop* T-shirts, and gather over there for the key swap."

Linley, the cameramen, and the girls all groaned at once.

Derek laughed. "You'll get dessert, but you have to work first. Those who are not involved in this scene— you better leave cake and coffee for us."

After they dressed and the cameras were set, the famed key swap began.

"OK, girls, you know the rules. You have two days and one long night to completely redo each other's room. You'll each have the help of a top-notch designer and our renowned carpenter. Each one of you gets to spend a cool thousand dollars on your friend's room. There's no peeking and absolutely no sharing of secrets." She paused and looked at each girl.

Sparkle. Don't forget to sparkle. Briana smiled even wider.

"Are you ready?"

"Yes!" The girls spoke in unison.

Linley took their keys and swapped them. "Then let the fun begin!"

The girls each crossed over in front of Linley and ran toward the other's house, overnight bag in hand.

"And . . . cut." Derek spoke to Linley. "I think that went well the first time, don't you?"

"How'd the girls look?" she asked.

"I thought they looked unusually good. Alert, not nervous, eager; but I didn't see any overacting." He paused and said, "I think it's a wrap."

"Oh, good," one of the cameramen said. "Dessert."

"I'll look at the footage back at the hotel tonight, but I think it works." He went over and got a cup of coffee and a piece of cake along with the cameramen.

"You girls seemed totally at ease," Linley said. "Because this is usually the first thing we shoot, we often have to do it over and over until our teens get comfortable with the camera."

"We've watched *Flip Flop* so many times, we could probably do that in our sleep," Chickie said.

When everyone had finished, Derek stood up. "OK, let's hit our respective sacks tonight. We'll see everyone in the morning at eight o'clock sharp. Nick, Trish—will you have a continental breakfast, or should we try to eat before gathering?"

"We've already got it planned. It'll all be out before eight," Chickie's dad said.

"Great. OK, everybody, sleep well and be ready to rock tomorrow," Derek said as he gathered his clipboard and notes.

❋　　　❋　　　❋

"I can't believe tonight will be our last night to sleep in the famous pretty pink princess bedroom," Briana said as she lounged across the bed.

"Oh, yeah, it's easy for you to tease about it. Millions of viewers all across America are going to see my bit of tweeny-bopper heaven. Can you imagine going to school next year—as a senior—and having everyone know about your Pretty Pony collection?"

"Maybe you should have considered this before you strong-armed our way onto *Flip Flop*."

"Actually, until the team gets here and everything gets under way, you really don't get how public this is, do you?"

"Are you talking about having our whole school out on the sidewalk between our houses? Actually, it's probably the whole town." Briana looked out the window into the darkness. "I wouldn't be surprised if some people were still hanging out there right now."

"Oh, stop. You're giving me the creeps."

"Isn't it different than you pictured?"

"When you watch it on TV it seems so homey—a teen and a designer tucked away in a bedroom, occasionally consulting with the carpenter or the host." Chickie ran her fingers through her hair. "Who ever pictured a small army that required food and lodging and, well, everything?"

"I know. And who ever thought there would be so many extra hands working on the rooms? No wonder they are so complex when they're done," Briana said.

"I worried that I wouldn't be able to do some of the stuff—like the sewing. Instead, we just have to do part of it. It's a big relief."

"We'd better try to do something to get to sleep—I'm still so keyed up I can hardly stand it."

"Me too, but Linley warned us about getting enough sleep."

Briana ran her hands over the bed frame. "After all

the time we've spent in this room, it seems strange that it will be a different room next time I spend the night."

"Tomorrow night will be the first time I'll ever have spent the night in your room, and the funny thing is, you won't even be there."

Briana froze. How awful did that sound? The first time. Didn't Chickie wonder why her best friend never invited her over?

"What about your secrets?" Chickie asked.

Briana sat up on the bed. She knew. All this time she knew everything. *How could I be so stupid as to think I had everything under control? Just like that, Chickie asks about my secret.*

"What's wrong? You look like you've seen a stalker out the window."

"It's what you said."

"What did I say?" Chickie tilted her head to the side. "Oh, you mean about what funny little secrets we'll find in your cave when we begin the load-out?" Chickie laughed. "I wouldn't worry; it can't be anything as embarrassing as my Pretty Ponies."

Of course. She meant girly secrets—not deep, dark, ruining-my-life secrets. Instead of relief, though, Briana just felt more jumpy.

"At least we never had any secrets from each other—best friends don't." Chickie climbed into bed. "I can't imagine how awful it would be if I were worried about you finding out about my princess alter ego."

Briana climbed into bed alongside her friend. The question that refused to go away was whether Chickie would still be her best friend when she found out that Briana had a whole life's worth of secrets.

The sound of the alarm clock jarred Briana awake. *What weird dreams.* She'd been doing the *Flip Flop* filming in a room—but it wasn't Chickie's room or any room she recognized. The cameras started to roll and someone—maybe Derek, but different—yelled "cut." She looked down and realized she didn't have any clothes on. Then she sort of ended up in another room, but it wasn't the right room. She couldn't find out where to go to get back to the filming.

Flip Flop! *Yikes!*

"Chickie, wake up. Today is Day One and we're sleeping through our alarm."

Chickie groaned and stretched. "What?"

"*Flip Flop.* Everyone's going to be out there waiting for us."

Chickie jumped out of bed. "Why didn't you wake me?"

Briana threw a pillow at her. "What do you think I just did? Do you want to shower first?"

"Sure. It's funny. I didn't think I'd be able to sleep at all for nervousness and anticipation. Instead, I slept right through the alarm."

"Me too. I dreamt strange dreams. I need to make sure I get my clothes on before the filming starts."

"Those kind of dreams, huh?"

Chickie went straight into the shower while Briana tidied up the room.

Why am I cleaning the room? Within two hours we are going to be ripping this room apart to the walls.

It was going to be so much fun. With Dad tied up in meetings in Las Vegas, she could just enjoy every

135

minute of the experience. How far was Las Vegas anyway? Briana thought she remembered that it was a nine-hour trip by car. Even if her dad did only today's meetings and got up early the next morning, the best he could do was catch the tail end. Everyone would be so busy, and he would have to have time to work up to a state of inebriation. The secret was probably safe.

After Chickie showered, Briana followed and she came out to the sound of the hair dryer.

"That shirt looks cute on you. I've often wondered if the color of the shirt has anything to do with the eventual color of the room?" Briana said.

"I don't think so. I've noticed it happening sometimes, but other times not. Are you trying to figure out if my rust-colored shirt means you are going to have an autumn-colored room?"

"I'll bet it has more to do with the time of year the show will air and how the colors look on us."

"You're probably right. That blue is about the color of your eyes. With your dark hair, you're going to look smashing on TV."

"I hope so. I'm trying not to think about how I look. It may make me too self-conscious. I think you're right, though, about them thinking about what looks best on us—your rust-colored shirt with your red hair and russet eyes couldn't be better. I don't think it's just what looks good on us, though. Certain colors seem to pop on screen."

"Isn't it so much fun to learn about the stuff behind the scenes? So much more goes into it than what we see on television," said Chickie.

"The only thing that would make this better would be if we could be together during the whole two days."

Briana took the hair dryer from Chickie. "To think that I'm going to be in this room for two days without you is so weird."

"I know. And to be having a slumber party with someone else in each other's rooms . . ." She didn't say anything until Briana finished drying her hair. "It seems strange to think of *Flip Flop*'s famous designers bringing their sleeping bags into our bedrooms for a slumber party, doesn't it?"

"We need to check the list one more time to make sure we have everything we need," Briana said, getting down to business. "I remember reading that they provide those cots you always see during the slumber party."

"My parents went over the instructions a million times. I can't believe we've left anything undone."

The girls finished getting ready. Both of them brushed their hair until it shined and applied makeup. Briana had teased Chickie about manicured nails, but she was happy they could start out looking good.

"Remember, they talked about continuity—making sure we keep things looking the same. This is supposed to be the same day as the key swap." Briana looked Chickie over. "Those are the same tennis shoes you wore yesterday, right?"

"Oops. Good save, Bree! I wore my Nikes yesterday but decided I didn't mind if these gym tennis shoes got paint on them." She took off her shoes and put the Nikes back on.

"I can't believe the day is here." Briana grabbed both of Chickie's hands and squeezed them.

"Do you think it would be dumb to pray before we start?" Chickie asked.

Briana was surprised. They prayed together at

church, but they'd never prayed just as friends. "No, it's not dumb. This is such a big thing—a special thing. You go, though, OK?" Briana felt a little funny.

"Dear God," Chickie began, "we are excited, scared, and—well, You know how we feel. We know we never would have gotten picked for *Flip Flop* if not for You. I mean, out of ten-thousand-some applicants? We know that You're doing something even though we don't know exactly what You are doing. Help us be natural and come across good on TV. Let us be good ambassadors for You even though we won't have an opportunity to talk about You or anything. Maybe You could just be there in our attitudes and our smiles." Chickie paused and shifted her weight. "Be with our families as they all work together. Thank You for bringing this into our neighborhood. Let the closeness stay. Help Briana's father not feel left out of the fun." She turned to Briana. "Do you want to add anything?"

"We love You, God," Briana said, then added, "even when You stretch us way outside what's comfortable for us."

"Amen," said Chickie.

"Amen." Briana breathed deeply. *Why do I feel as if I've just had a deep drink of water? I feel so much calmer.* She let go of Chickie's hands. "So, this is it."

"Yep. This is it."

As they walked out to the canteen to get some breakfast, she felt as if she and Chickie had just taken their friendship to a deeper level. *Is it weird to pray with a friend?* It felt weird at first, but something happened as they stood there. It didn't feel weird when they finished.

✺   ✺   ✺

"Remember absolutely every tiny detail to tell me tomorrow night, OK?" Chickie asked as they got close to the point they'd have to separate.

"OK, team. Gather over here." Derek motioned for everyone to gather at the tables in the makeshift canteen. "If you're late"—he lowered his head to look out with hooded eyes at Chris—"grab a cup of coffee, some fruit, and a Danish; and sit down over here."

Everyone sat or stood around. Briana waved at Mom, who sat near Suzanne. Briana wondered if they had worked into the night.

Petra and Claire sat together with Joe and Sebastian; plans laid out on the table. Chris got his breakfast and joined them. The cameramen sat next to Linley and Derek's assistant. Mr. and Mrs. Wells presided over the breakfast buffet, and Geoff manned the garbage can.

Linley got up to stand next to Derek and looked over his shoulder at the clipboard. She looked up. "Chickie, Briana, you girls look good. Stand up and let us see you."

Both girls pushed back their chairs and stood up.

"I'm glad we went with that rust for you, Chickie. I think it looks better than the orange we originally planned," Linley said. "The camera should love both of you."

Derek looked back at his clipboard. "Jack, you're going to be mostly filming Petra, right?"

He nodded.

"Bree has a very expressive face. Be sure to try to get in tight during surprises or during disappointments."

"While we finish up here, you guys go set up the overhead cams and get your lighting set. We'll be there in forty-five minutes. Plan to do Petra's paint reveal first, Jack; then do her instructions at Camp Carpentry." He turned to the other cameraman. "We'll do the opposite for you. Do the Camp Carpentry footage first; then do the reveal." He turned to the girls. "Much of our planning has to do with keeping the teams separate and keeping things moving. We wouldn't want Petra hanging around Camp Carpentry while Claire is talking over plans."

He pointed at Sebastian. "While the filming is going on at Camp Carpentry, you and Joe will help out with the painting, since Chris will be holding court."

Chris made a face. They seemed to love to tease Chris since he was a bit of a prima donna.

"Sebastian, you work with Petra and Bree—Joe with Claire and Chickie."

"One thing I need to repeat," Linley said. "Even though we have a little more help behind the scenes than what appears on camera, and even though we may shoot scenes out of order, most parts of the show are exactly as you see them. One of the most exciting elements is the sense of surprise." She paused. "If any of the details are revealed before the formal reveal, it shows in the emotional punch of the reveal. The show falls flat if the reveal is not authentic."

Derek nodded and waited for her to finish.

"We tease a lot on set. We want this show to be fun and filled with drama, but we are serious about creating unforgettable designs and making the kind of television that keeps people glued to *Flip Flop* week after week," Linley continued.

"We have one of the most loyal fan bases on television," Derek said.

"So when we say you are not to know anything about each other's rooms, we mean it." Linley walked over to where the girls were sitting. "Bree, your mom will be in the sewing center. Chickie, Sebastian will know everything that's going on. Both your parents will be sleeping in their own homes and will know what's going on in your rooms. We ask you to give us your word not to attempt to find out any details of your own room's progress. Promise?"

Chickie spoke up. "We promise. We want this to be the best episode ever."

"Besides," Bree said, "it will be hard to be thinking about our own rooms with all the work we'll be doing. I promise as well."

"And all you helpers—this is one of the key elements of the show." Linley sat down.

"OK. Thanks, Linley. We'll break for lunch and dinner on a staggered schedule." Derek handed schedules to the designers and Linley. "Drinks and snacks will be set up in the kitchens of each house for everyone working there. Arrange your breaks as needed. Linley will meet with each designer starting at about three o'clock to see where you are budget-wise and to film her money worries footage with you."

He turned to his assistant. "Have I forgotten anything?"

She looked at the clipboard, flipping pages. "Everyone has the staggered schedule for tomorrow too, right?"

"That's right. No more breakfast together; no more meetings together. Check your schedules. Tomorrow afternoon, Linley will let you know when she'll do her deadline worries footage." He turned toward the girls.

"We always show the stretch of the budget constraint and the time crunch on camera. It adds to the dramatic tension, but let me tell you—it's not hard to come up with those every week. Each time we film those, they are real worries.

"OK. I'll be wandering around. Linley will guide things along. The cameramen may suggest scenes as well. There should be times on your schedules to get the girls into the sewing center and into Camp Carpentry."

The assistant spoke up. "Remember to watch those schedules, Suzanne and Joe. You need to clean up one room's projects before the other girl comes in."

"I want great shots of the girls at the sewing machine and with power tools," Derek said.

"Petra, Claire, you can go get set up for the meet and greet and the paint reveal." The designers gave each other a high five and took off to their rooms.

"Girls," Derek said, "you've met your designers a number of times so far, but we purposely have not let them interact with you. When you go into the room, you'll be meeting them as if it's for the first time. It almost will be, since we've purposely kept the designers low-key until now. You'll only meet them in full personality as you work with them. Before this *Flip Flop* is over, you'll have either made a friend or, in rare cases, you'll hate their guts."

"Not with Petra and Claire," Chris said with a wink, "though I won't say which of our other designers sometimes elicits that reaction."

Derek looked at his clipboard one more time. "OK, let the *Flip Flop* begin. Bree and Chickie, go and meet your designers."

Moroccan Sunrise

11

Briana, come in, come in." Petra greeted her warmly. "I've heard your friends call you Bree. May I call you that?"

"Petra. Hello." Briana was all too aware of the cameras rolling. "Yes, please call me Bree— much shorter."

"So are you ready to say good-bye to— umm, what would you call this style?"

"Chickie's been ready for years. She calls it her pretty pink princess room." Briana laughed. "I think she feels a little uncomfortable having

America see this room. She wanted me to stress to everyone that this is *so* not her."

Petra's whole face opened into a smile. "That's the neat thing about *Flip Flop*. We usually come into a room that was decorated by a parent right after their child outgrew the nursery. Too often, there's a huge disconnect between the room and our teen."

"You've met Chickie. . . ."

"Yes, and this room does not represent the complexity of your friend. Tell us a little about her and what you would like to see us do for her room."

"Hmmm. Chickie's a lot like the way she looks. She's delicate; she loves detail and tiny things, but she says she longs for warmth and coziness. I think she's hoping for a sophisticated room."

"Good description, Bree. I'm heading the same direction as you. I took one look at Chickie's burnished hair and brown eyes, and I knew which way I wanted to go." Petra took her by the hand and pulled her to the other side of the room. "Come sit with me on my magic carpet." She pulled Briana down onto an old Persian carpet. The whole center was worn to the threads.

"Are you planning on putting this carpet in the room?" Briana couldn't keep the doubt out of her voice.

"Yes, but not like you think." Petra laughed. "All will be revealed."

Briana could tell she was really going to like working with Petra. Funny that she'd hardly noticed before now. Once her personality came out, she lit up the room.

"I'm calling this design Moroccan Sunrise. What do you think?"

"Hmmm. Well, I'm not so fond of themed rooms. . . ."

"I know what you mean by 'themed room,' and this room is not going to be dominated by a slavish attempt to create a theme. Don't worry. I just like to name my rooms for the look and the feel. Moroccan for the style; sunrise for the color."

"It sounds interesting." Briana knew she couldn't keep the question out of her voice. She noticed the cameraman angling in for a tight shot, and remembered that Derek wanted him to get any emotions on her face.

"Well, speaking of color—are you ready to see our paint colors?"

"Yes!"

Petra pried open the first can and lifted the lid with a flourish. "So, what do you think of this?"

"You really want to know?" Briana looked down at the watery-looking olive green stuff. The camera moved in on her face. "Is this paint? It sort of looks like algae-filled pond water."

Petra laughed so hard she made a snorting noise. "Oh, cut! Be sure to cut before that inelegant snort, please." She turned to Briana. "That was perfect. Your face says it all. Keep being honest, and the camera will catch all the emotions. OK, now for the other paints."

Petra looked up at the camera and smiled as she pried open the second can. "What do you think of this color?" It was a golden yellow.

"That's pretty . . . sunny."

"Right. I call it sunrise because it's golden yellow tinged with the warmth of red."

Briana laughed. "I like it even better now. I love the way you describe things almost better than the way they look."

"I'd better keep talking, then. OK, here's our last color." She pried open a quart of metallic gold.

"Wow. The room's gonna bling!"

"Good description. We will also be using gold leaf— well, faux gold leaf—so expect real *bling, bling.*"

"This sounds like fun, though I still can't figure out what we are going to do with the algae-colored paint."

"OK, let me tell you what we're doing to the walls and we will go from there. See this paper?" She unrolled a thick white roll of wallpaper. "It's not normal paper; it's called Lincrusta."

"Look, it has a design embossed in it. Cool."

"We'll use regular wallpaper paste and hang this paper. Are you good on a ladder?"

Briana grimaced. "Does *Flip Flop* have good insurance?"

Petra laughed. "Maybe we'll make Linley and Chris help us. After we hang the wallpaper, we'll roller the gold-colored paint all over the surface."

"We're going to paint the wallpaper?"

"Yes. That's how Lincrusta is finished—with paint. After the paint dries, we'll brush on your favorite algae green. It's actually a wood stain. As we brush on a section, we'll take a soft rag and take the stain off. It'll stay in the recessed places, and the gold will show through on the raised parts. It will end up looking like old moroccan leather."

"I think Chickie will love this. I've been so anxious to get rid of my dark cave, but Chickie grew tired of her white furniture and wanted something warm and exotic."

"So far, so good, then, right?"

The cameraman put down his camera. "Good job. I think that went well. Petra, we have to go out and do the Chris thing, right? I think Sebastian's coming in to help hang the paper, but that's a job. Maybe Linley can help too."

"OK. We'll see who we can round up. We need to have the paper hung by lunchtime and the paint done by dinner. We're going to hold off on the stain until tomorrow morning, or we couldn't bear to sleep in the room tonight."

After that, the work just kept up steadily. Briana was surprised to find that with good instructions, she was not bad. She ended up with the job of rolling out strips of Lincrusta, carefully matching the designs, and cutting. When Petra came back, she applied the paste to the back of the strips, and Sebastian hung the Lincrusta, strip after strip. Briana liked working with Sebastian and Petra, and as they joked and talked, they began to feel like a team.

"OK, Sebastian," Petra said as the cameraman came in. "Next time you get off the ladder, we'll let Bree climb up and pretend she's hanging the wallpaper."

"Oh, this should be good," Sebastian said as he finished smoothing the piece from center up and center down.

Petra gave him a swat on the shoulder. "Be nice." She finished brushing paste and folding the piece for Briana. "Don't forget, Sebastian, you are not here; so don't laugh or make a noise when the camera is rolling."

Briana slid the smoothing brush into the back pocket of her jeans and climbed halfway up the ladder, trying to remember how Sebastian did it. Petra handed up the piece of paper. "You rolling, Jack?"

"Yup."

Briana laid the sticky side of the paper against the seam of the other paper to the left, sliding it up and down until she matched the design.

"How are you coming in here?" Linley asked.

Briana started. She hadn't heard Linley come in. The ladder wobbled and Briana's hands went out to try to catch her balance. Petra managed to steady the ladder, but when Briana threw her hands up, the wallpaper began sliding down the wall.

Briana turned and smiled at the camera. "Fine." She looked over at Sebastian. He had his hand clasped over his mouth, but he was bent over from laughter. Both Linley and Petra watched the piece continue its slow-motion slide.

With a straight face, Linley asked, "So, how're you doing for time?"

That was all it took. The whole room burst into laughter as Derek yelled, "Cut."

"Thank goodness I had the camera on a tripod," said Jack. "I laughed so hard at her 'fine,' while in the background we could see the ladder wobbling and the wallpaper sagging off the wall."

"Has all the footage been that good in here?" asked Derek.

"Close to it," said the cameraman.

"Sebastian, will you please fix this for us before the paste dries?" Petra said.

Briana managed to get down the ladder.

As Sebastian retrieved the pile of wallpaper on the floor, he turned to Briana. "Out of my way, little lady," he said in a John Wayne voice. "Let a man do it."

Petra rolled her eyes. "I won't hold it against you, Bree, if you kick the ladder by mistake."

"I'm getting out of here. You guys are having altogether too much fun," Derek said. "Hey, Petra—before Jack goes out to Camp Carpentry, why don't you clue Bree in on the other design elements on camera?"

"Will do."

"Oh, and Bree," Derek said as he walked out the door, "you have a big glob of wallpaper paste on your cheek."

Sebastian never turned around, but Briana could see by the shaking of his shoulders that he was laughing again.

"OK," Petra said. "Sebastian, you keep going there. We're running short of time. We'll move over here on that kilim."

"Kilim?" Bree had no idea what she was talking about.

"The Persian rug. OK, let's roll."

She turned to Briana with her wallpaper brush in hand. "We've been hanging wallpaper for what seems like forever. Aren't you the least bit curious about what else we're going to be doing?"

Briana groaned. "You mean there's more?"

Petra laughed. "Oh, we haven't even begun to work—that was just an appetizer. So, you said Chickie was sick of her furniture, right?"

"Are we going to paint it?"

"Some of it. But see this bed?"

"Yes."

"We're tossing it out." Petra smiled. "We are going to make a bed fit for a Moroccan princess."

"Oh, please don't use the p-word. Poor Chickie lived in a princess bedroom for too long."

"Picture this: a wooden platform suspended by four

gold chains from the ceiling with gold rope entwined down the chain length ending in these massive gold tassels at the corners of the platform." She picked up four huge metallic gold tassels from a stack of supplies at her side.

"OK, I'm speechless," Briana said. "You mean her bed is going to be hanging from the ceiling?"

"Yes."

"And will it hold the weight of Chickie and even a couple other girls if we have a sleepover here?"

"Absolutely. We'll get Carpenter Chris in here to drill through the ceiling joists in the attic and install an eyebolt to attach the chains."

"And the mattress will go on top of the platform?"

"Exactly, but you haven't heard it all." Petra smiled and pointed toward the rug under them. "I found this worn carpet in a secondhand shop for next to nothing. We are going to add matching fringe to the long sides, and we are going to cut eighteen inches off all four sides of the carpet and staple it to the sides of the platform like a fringed carpet skirt."

Briana clapped her hands. "Oh, Petra, I get it! You're making a flying carpet. That is too cool!"

"Oh, how I love it when my teen decorator is in tune." Petra continued, "We'll leave the red pine floors since the warm color will come alive in our Moroccan room."

"So once the walls are done, we'll be able to move on to the furniture?"

"Not quite. See the ceiling up there?"

"Yeah."

"We need to create a sunrise sky framed by gilt moldings. We'll paint the ceiling our golden color, lightly rag on some of our green stain to give it a patina of age, and then we'll go to work on the woodwork."

"Woodwork?" This sounded like a lot of work. Briana laughed. A lot of work for Sebastian. "Oh, you mean Carpenter Chris?" She tried to get a gleam in her eye. It was always fun to play the flirt-with-Chris game on camera. Especially since Sebastian was just across the room hanging the rest of the wallpaper.

"Look at this great fiberboard lattice I found. I think it's supposed to be for speaker fronts or something. Anyway, we are going to paint it metallic gold and put it over the whole ceiling, so it looks as if we are looking through a metal screen to the morning sky."

"I love the design of the lattice—those petal-like openings. It does look exotic. I can't believe it's . . . well, it's cardboard, isn't it?"

"Just about. At the top of the wall I have Chris scheduled to install massive crown molding." She reached down and picked up a piece of white molding. "It will paint up just like wood, but it's really polystyrene. Much cheaper and easier to install. We'll be painting this our wall color, but then applying this faux gold leaf to the surface."

"The way you describe it, I can't wait to see it, but—" Briana grimaced and massaged her temples. "Can we get it all done? It sounds like a lot of work."

"Am I giving you a headache, Bree?" Petra laughed. "We may have to work long into the night, but I've never left a half-finished room yet."

Petra smiled into the camera for a minute. ". . . And cut."

"Oh, Petra. It sounds beyond cool. Chickie's going to faint when she sees this."

"Believe it or not, I'm done." Sebastian smoothed the last piece of Lincrusta down. "Do we really have to get this painted before we can eat lunch?"

Petra checked her schedule. "No, we just need to finish painting before dinner. Let's go before the Harris house team gets over there. I heard Trish and Nick were doing tacos and salad for lunch."

"Man, wait till you taste my mom's tacos. I was afraid the camera would pick up my rumbling stomach."

Briana walked with Sebastian over to the canteen. "Are you tired?"

"That was a lot of work in a short time, but with so many hands and so much laughter, it went fast." He flexed his shoulders. "I'll bet I'm going to be sore tomorrow from all that papering with my hands over my head."

"I can't believe you can do all that."

"It's shocking me too," he said. "I've been doing my share of praying that I could accomplish each task they give me."

"You make it look easy."

"So far, if I do exactly what they say and don't try to cut any corners, it's working. Nobody's as surprised as me, though."

"Really?"

"I've been so afraid that someone would find out I don't know what I'm doing."

"Me too. You take something like this on and it looks overwhelming."

"Yeah, it's like that elephant thing."

Elephant thing? What is he talking about? Briana stopped for a minute to try to catch a breath. *Not my elephant in the living room . . .*

"You know. The question is, 'How do you eat an elephant?' The answer is, 'One bite at a time.'"

Briana took a deep breath. *How many elephant metaphors are there, anyway? You've got to stop overreacting. Everything's going smoothly, and Dad's probably sitting in meeting after meeting in Las Vegas, and—*

"Where did you go, Bree? Did I gross you out with elephant cuisine?"

"Sorry. There's so much going on; I'm feeling a bit overwhelmed myself."

Sebastian laughed. "One bite at a time, then."

The afternoon flew by. Briana tried to remember everything so she could tell Chickie later, but the jobs just came one on top of the other. They worked on the walls for much of the time, then helped as Chris and Joe installed the painted gridwork. Briana painted walls and gold-leafed molding, sanded furniture, and talked to the camera.

"Bree," said Petra as she came up behind her, "are you as tired as I am?"

"I don't know. Do you feel like you could sleep on the top step of the ladder?"

"Let's go down to the kitchen and have a cold drink and put our feet up. What do you say?"

"Will we have to get up again?"

"Uh-oh. We're not even halfway through the room's makeover."

Jack stopped them as he got off his cell phone. "Can I have you wait for just a couple minutes? Linley's on her way to talk to Bree."

Petra and Bree groaned in unison.

"You go down and start," Bree said to Petra as Linley walked in.

"Come down as soon as you're done."

"I was just wondering how things are going," Linley asked as the camera rolled.

"I think they're going well, but with so many jobs going at the same time, who knows?"

"Have you wondered about what's going on at your house?"

"Not really. I haven't had time to wonder what's going on right here in this room." That amazed Briana. It was true. Normally she worried about everything at her house. Where was Dad? Was he upset? Had he gone out? Had he come back? *For the last twenty-four hours, I've worked hard and had more fun than I can remember having in ages.*

"Just as much work's being done in your room, you know."

"Tell me that Chickie's just as tired as me."

Linley laughed. "So what's the worst thing you can imagine happening over at your house?"

Oh, you don't want to know the answer to that, Linley, but I know you mean design-wise. . . . "I guess anything dark, too bold, or in-your-face. I mean, I've lived in that dark room for many years—my cave—I'd like the opposite now."

"OK, good. Go and take your break now."

When Briana got downstairs, the whole Wells house crew had gathered with the exception of Linley. Sebastian asked her how the elephant was going down, which piqued everyone's interest. He had to explain his eating-the-elephant image.

It was fun to just kick back and talk, snack, and drink for a few minutes.

Before many minutes passed, though, Linley came

down and looked at her watch in that characteristic pose. "I'm getting worried about time," she said. Since the cameras were not running, they knew her worry was for real.

"OK," Petra said. "Bree, you and Jack head over to the sewing center to get some shots of you on the sewing machine and manning an iron. Hurry back when you are done."

"No rest for the wicked," Sebastian said as he smiled that melt-their-hearts smile. And people thought Chris was a hottie?

"Speaking of wicked, I hope your wicked sense of humor holds out till nightfall, Mr. Sebastian. We are going to push hard before and after dinner."

Briana chuckled the whole way over to her garage. How fun was this?

"Wait here," Jack said. "Let me make sure the coast is clear."

A couple of minutes later, he opened the side door to let her in. She saw Suzanne and her mother working on separate machines, stitching more of the gorgeous gilt-decorated fabrics she saw yesterday. "Hi, Suzanne. Hi, Mom. I'm supposed to do some sewing and ironing here for the camera."

She expected her mother to make some funny remark about her skills, or just to raise her eyebrows, but Mom kept her head bent over her machine. *Oh, no!* Briana recognized that body language immediately. *What happened? What did she hear?*

"Come sit at my machine," Suzanne said, sliding out of the chair. "Oh, wait; let me change the stitch length to a basting stitch just in case I have to rip it out."

Mom managed a tight little laugh, but Briana recognized it. *She's running on nerves.*

"OK, just show me what to do." Briana did exactly as Suzanne said, and she actually ended up sewing a reasonably straight seam for the camera. Next she went to the ironing table and did some pressing for the camera. At least she'd done that before. *Yeah, baby, I must really be an actress. I mean, I can see that something is crashing down around me and still smile and joke for the camera. Weird.*

"OK, I think that will work," Suzanne said. "I'm going into the kitchen to take a break. Join me, Anna, as soon as Briana leaves."

Jack left to go back to the Wells house, leaving Mom and Briana alone in the sewing center.

"What's wrong, Mom?" Briana whispered.

"How do you know something's wrong?"

"Oh, Mom. After all these years, I can pick up the slightest sign. What happened?"

"Your dad called to say he feels left out of all the excitement. He managed to finish up the meetings." Mom showed no emotion at all. She'd become an expert at hiding her reactions.

"So is he on his way?"

"He said he wanted to kick back a little first, and then when he felt rested, he'd start home."

Briana felt the danger signs go off in her head. Certain words set off the sirens: kick back . . . rest . . . driving afterward. "When do you think he'll arrive?" She couldn't keep the quiver out of her voice.

"You need to let me handle this, Briana. I can tell you are getting upset. You won't be able to be yourself on camera if you're worried."

"I can't help myself. This is what I worried about the whole time Chickie talked about doing this. Dad will come home ranting and raving. Can you imagine what he'll say when he sees the garage? Then he'll come barging in the house. Chickie and Claire are sleeping or working upstairs, Mom."

"Now don't borrow trouble, honey."

"I've never needed to borrow trouble. It's always found me. It even wakes me out of a sound sleep."

"If Dad took an hour to relax, he could be home about two in the morning, probably later."

"The thing that worries me the most is that I've never told a single soul about this, including my best friend, who thinks she knows everything there is to know about me."

"That's good, though. Our business is our business. I've never wanted people knowing what goes on in our house. We've always been very private people."

Briana didn't want to dig deeper into that attitude right now. She just knew she felt that it was time to stop covering up. Would her dad ever have to change if they helped him keep on living with that problem? *Who knows?*

"I need to get back. Come get me if you need me tonight, OK?"

"Briana, I can handle this. You go and have fun."

"There is no way I can have fun with this hanging over us. I'll do my best to act like I'm having fun, but . . ."

Briana walked over to Chickie's room. Whatever had made her think she could pull this off?

Oh, no," Petra said as they came into the canteen. "Not grilled steaks and barbecued corn. I'm going to gain five pounds on this Mercey Springs *Flip Flop.*"

Briana smiled as she filled her plate.

"OK," Petra said, "spill. You've been subdued ever since break this afternoon. Luckily enough, we got tons of vibrant footage this morning, but the camera will pick up the change."

"I'm sorry," Briana said. "I must be winding down. Maybe eating dinner will pump me back up."

They took their plates and went over to sit at the end of one of the tables. Traffic in front of the green had finally slowed down some. Ever since the *Flip Flop* truck and signage was set up, the crowds had been swelling. The teams had all learned to ignore the people and concentrate on the task at hand. For the most part, Briana had been unaware.

Now as she looked at the cars slowing down to watch and saw the people standing on the sidewalk, she wondered what kind of show they might get to see courtesy of her father. *What is wrong with me? I'm losing my grip. Not only did I let the lid of my own Pandora's box be vulnerable, but it may very well fly open in front of the biggest audience on cable TV, not to mention the entire populace of Mercey Springs. After all these years of managing to keep all my secrets under control, what happened?*

"Briana? Where did you go?"

"Yikes, sorry. Zoning out."

"OK, why not tell Auntie Petra what's on your mind? Did you have a misunderstanding with Sebastian?"

That came out of the blue. Briana blinked hard. "Why would you say that?"

"Maybe I misunderstood, but there seems to be a little electricity between the two of you." Petra watched her face.

"No. Maybe. I don't know, but he's my friend and has only been funny and helpful and . . . no, not Sebastian."

Petra laughed. "OK. I'd call that conflicted about Sebastian." She put a hand over Briana's hand. "For what it's worth, I'm impressed with him. I've never seen such a skilled helper hired locally. And I've done a lot of shows."

"He surprised me," Briana admitted.

"Plus, he seems to be deep—a man of faith. I love that. Did you notice that if he comes to a meal and misses having Nick pray, he bows his head quietly by himself?"

"I hadn't noticed, but a while back he talked to me about how he examined his childhood faith—the inherited church stuff from his parents—and examined it hard and made it his own. Cool, huh?" Briana peeled back the darkened husks from her roasted corn. "Why did you point out his faith?"

"I guess because it is so important to me. I've walked the same journey as Sebastian but from a different vantage point. Being an artist, I thought it looked more artsy to explore all religions. I wanted something with the pacifism of a Gandhi, the mystery of a High Mass, the mercy of the Salvation Army, the body awareness of yoga, the—well, you get it."

"It sure sounds eclectic," Briana said.

"I grew up in a messed-up family—now they call it dysfunctional. I guess it felt normal to have a messed-up sort of spirituality." Petra took a bite of salad and chewed slowly.

Briana did not interrupt. She wanted to hear more about Petra. So far, her designer had spent most of her time trying to draw the best out of everyone else on the set. She seemed to be so intuitive, to watch faces and to be able to head off problems. She took care of everyone else, but she didn't reveal much about herself.

"One day, when I was doing yoga and trying to 'get in touch with my creative self,' I felt a huge empty space in my life—a hole that refused to be filled no matter how hard I worked at it. Once I admitted to my emptiness, I went on my own search to fill it. I tried everything short of what I saw as organized religion."

"Is that where you finally went?"

"A friend gave me a Bible as a gift, knowing I was into spirituality. She had no idea it was more than another ancient text." She stopped and put down her fork. "The Bible opened my eyes. Do you know what my name means?"

"Doesn't it mean the rock, like Peter?"

"Yes. How funny that my parents named me the rock and I was the wishy-washiest person I knew. That's what I love about God. He always knew I'd be a rock." Petra looked down at her plate, which had been barely touched. "Am I talking your ear off? I didn't mean to go on about me."

"No, please don't stop. I've been on my own journey, and I love hearing God stories."

"It didn't take long for me to realize that my emptiness was not for a form of spirituality; it was for a person. Reading the Bible clarified things for me. By the time I pieced together the whole thing—our sin separating us from God, and the bridge He used to reach us—I couldn't help but see the truth. The bridge, His own Son, Jesus, became the center of life and filled that hole."

Briana took a deep breath in through her nose. "When you tell it, it makes so much sense. I wish I had a magic moment like that."

"I don't tell my story often because I know God draws us to Himself in so many different ways." She laughed. "Besides, when I get going I worry that I'm going to sound like what my dad used to call a Bible-thumper. I don't want to scare people away from Jesus by my clumsy way of connecting to them."

"No. I loved your story," Briana said.

"How about your story?"

"Well, I started going to church with Chickie's family a few years back, and I knew it was true right from the beginning. What I heard, I accepted."

"Wow. The gift of faith?" Petra asked.

"Maybe. But I don't know that I've really let it change my life. I'm not sure. I mean, Sebastian talked to me about letting God work in my life instead of trying so hard. That's been knocking around my brain in the days since then."

Petra chuckled. "I'll bet that's hard. Since I've gotten to know you, I can already see you are a high-control person. Letting go may be the hardest thing you ever do in your life."

Derek came into the canteen. "Eat up, Wells house team. The Harris house people tell me they are starving."

"Oops. I talked your ear off, Bree. I guess I just see that you and I are kindred spirits." She stuffed some more food in her mouth. "Come on; let's take those brownies and ice cream to go."

They put in another good four hours of work in the evening. They'd decided to put their pj's on at ten o'clock.

"I think we're in good shape for tomorrow," Petra said into the camera in response to Linley's worried question. "First thing tomorrow morning, we are going to stain our Lincrusta walls, put the hardware back on our freshly painted furniture, hang the bed, install the draperies and bed hangings, load in the room, place the rugs, and—"

Briana laughed. "So you mean we should give up sleep at our slumber party tonight."

They all laughed together as the cameraman gave the hand signal that he had enough.

"OK. Everybody out," Petra said. "Bree and I are going to get comfy—as comfy as one can get when they know they'll be lounging in front of millions of viewers."

"That makes me feel at ease," Bree said.

"Jack can come back and do some filming until eleven; then we want the overhead cam shut off and Jack out of here."

"I'll be more than happy to go back to the hotel to catch a few hours' sleep," he said.

After they put on their pajamas, fuzzy slippers, and robes, and set up their cots and sleeping bags, the cameras came back in. First they filmed a craft segment showing the two of them turning plain old lampshades into fringed, gold-leafed shades. Briana couldn't believe the things she'd learned to do. And she wasn't half bad at them either.

She tried to be natural and laugh, to somehow recapture the fun of the morning, but she could feel the tenseness in her shoulders. She kept listening for any sounds in the night. All she could hear was the sound of saws and sanders at Camp Carpentry and a few cars still slowing down as they drove by. Her mom had been right; their house was isolated. You couldn't hear a sound. There was no telling what could be happening over there.

Stop it. It's too early anyway. God grant me serenity.

"You've gone quiet again, Bree," Petra said to the camera. "I know what's on your mind."

I bet you don't.

"You're thinking about Chickie and Claire having a slumber party in your room, aren't you?"

Briana smiled. She could play along—this was safe and usually worked for the camera. "You don't think they've given me a themed room, like, say, fifties sock hop with 45s plastered all over the walls?"

"Uh-oh, are you saying you'd hate that?"

Briana made a gagging gesture. There, that should give the camera something less depressing than her tension-creased forehead.

"Did you know that Claire was a world-renowned calligrapher before she joined *Flip Flop*?"

Briana hadn't known that. Her raised eyebrows were authentic.

"She doesn't often incorporate her art into her rooms because most rooms do not need words to make a design statement, but I could see a sweetshop with a jukebox and famous fifties top-thirty songs lettered across the walls."

"I sincerely hope Claire can't see that," Briana said with heartfelt sincerity, her hands clasped across her chest. "I'm going to be a good sport, and I'll probably be like all the other *Flip Flop*pers and love my room even if it's the exact opposite of what I think, but I do love simplicity."

"Great. Perfect." She turned to Jack. "Now, shut off the cameras and run. Let's all try to get to sleep before we turn into pumpkins."

After he left, they each took their turn in the bathroom, then turned out the light and climbed into their sleeping bags.

"Can you believe this?" Petra said into the dark room. "I'm thirty-two years old and still sleeping in a sleeping bag at a slumber party each week."

"At least yours is a designer sleeping bag," Briana

said. "I had to borrow Geoff's Spongebob Squarepants sleeping bag. How sad is that?"

The night had finally quieted, save for the occasional car that drove by. Sebastian and Joe were sleeping over at Camp Carpentry. According to Sebastian, that was how it originally got its name. On one of the first episodes, after a couple of expensive power tools disappeared, Derek decided the helpers could double as security in good weather. During bad weather, they hired security.

They'd only been lying there for fifteen minutes or so when Briana heard a faint knock at the door. She sat up immediately, every muscle tense and her heart thumping so hard, her chest hurt. She knew it. She'd always known it. It was bound to happen.

"Who is it?" Petra asked.

"Sebastian. May I have a quick word with Bree?"

Petra got up and switched on the light, putting her robe over her pajamas.

Briana did the same without thinking. *I probably should have put my clothes on, so I could go over there and . . . and what?* What could she do? Why did she always think she could fix things? *Help me, Jesus.*

Petra opened the door.

Sebastian seemed embarrassed. "Bree, your mom asked me to tell you that your dad didn't get on the road like he thought. He decided to relax awhile first?" Sebastian said that with a question, like he couldn't understand why he had to come all the way over to give this information. "He won't be home until sometime tomorrow evening."

Briana could barely catch her breath. "Thank you, Sebastian. Thank you." *Thank You, Jesus.* "Tell my mother thank you for letting me know. Oh, thanks so much, Sebastian." She knew she was babbling. She couldn't help herself. All the tightness in her chest—tightness that had kept building since she talked to Mom—it all seemed to unwind at once. She wanted to hug Sebastian.

"Um—you're welcome?" He looked confused. "I'd better get back. Good night, Petra. Night, Bree. Sorry to disturb you." He backed out of the door.

Briana sat down on her cot since her knees felt wobbly with relief. As she took deep breaths, she could feel the raggedness of her breathing. *If I don't get myself under control, I'm going to burst out in tears.*

"OK, this is a slumber party; let's talk." Petra sat on the edge of her cot.

"No, I'm OK. You know how it is to be startled out of sleep."

"Except you weren't sleeping. I could hear you over there worrying."

"I'm fine now."

"OK, I'm butting in here, big-sister style. See this?" She held up Briana's "Serenity Prayer" card. "Claire found it under your mattress. It was so worn she knew it was a precious part of you, so she gave it to me to give to you while you were going through this flip-flop. I decided to wait until the end."

Briana didn't say anything.

"You noticed how good I am at reading faces and understanding people. You're the same way. One of the things I noticed about you was how tense you were around your dad at the B-roll shoot. Always watching."

"Did it show?" Briana thought her secrets were so well hidden.

"It wouldn't have shown to anyone else. When

Claire handed me your prayer, I knew for sure that we were kindred spirits in more ways than one. Did you know the 'Serenity Prayer' has been a lifeline for alcoholics and families of substance abusers for years?"

"No." What was Petra trying to say?

"I told you I had a messed-up family. Alcohol abuse caused most of the chaos."

"You?" Briana didn't know why it surprised her. She knew she wasn't the only one keeping secrets; it was just that—well, she didn't know why it seemed so surprising.

"I recognized the tension tonight and knew you were fearful of having a scene develop. When Sebastian gave you that news and I saw your reaction, well . . ."

"I couldn't help myself. You have no idea how I dreaded my secret coming out."

"Boy, do I hear you. My freedom came when I stopped trying so hard to keep all the secrets to myself. I don't mean I told everyone I knew, but I eventually told trusted friends; and slowly I began to realize that I couldn't change other people, and I wasn't responsible for their choices." She went over and sat next to Briana, putting an arm around her shoulders. "After I came to know Jesus, I realized He's the One who can do the changing. It took a huge burden off me."

"I've begun to call on Him too, but I'm still trying to control things. That's why the prayer means so much to me."

"Did you know you don't have the entire prayer?"

"What do you mean?"

"You only have the first four lines. There's more." Petra got up. "I have a gift for you. I planned to give it to you as a good-bye gift, but now is as good a time as any."

Petra handed Briana a beautiful whitewashed frame with the whole "Serenity Prayer."

"Did Claire do this?" Briana asked. It was written in beautiful calligraphic text in soft tan ink on an ivory background.

"Yes. She did it during her afternoon break. Isn't it a work of art?"

Briana hugged Petra. "I will treasure it forever."

"I'm going to bed, or we'll have our first failure tomorrow. Good night, friend."

"I'm going to go out on the landing where there's more light and read the whole prayer. I'll be right in afterward."

As she got into the light, Briana read the words:

> God grant me the serenity
> To accept the things I cannot change;
> Courage to change the things I can,
> And wisdom to know the difference.
> Living one day at a time;
> Enjoying one moment at a time;
> Accepting hardship as the pathway to peace.
> Taking, as He did, this sinful world
> As it is, not as I would have it.
> Trusting that He will make all things right
> If I surrender to His Will;
> That I may be reasonably happy in this life,
> And supremely happy with Him forever in
>   the next.
> Amen.
>   —Reinhold Niebuhr

Forget the key swap of yesterday. Petra had given her the real key tonight.

The Reveal

13

If anything, Day Two went even faster than Day One.

Briana hadn't gotten a full night's sleep, but what she did get was so restful that she faced the day with a light heart.

She couldn't help but think about the words she received last night from Petra. The second half of the prayer offered so much wisdom. Today she focused on the words, "Living one day at a time; enjoying one moment at a time."

"Gather around, Wells house team," Linley

said. "It's time to do the panic scene. I'm guessing it's not going to be hard to elicit believable panic."

The cameraman gave the signal.

"Petra," Linley said, coming into the room and looking around, "is there any way you can get this all pulled together?"

"We're waiting on Carpenter Chris to come hang our platform." She took her hand, palm up, and swept it in an arc toward the walls. "I know it looks like a mess, but we have the walls and ceiling done, window treatment and bed hangings—I mean, it's not as bad as it looks."

Briana looked doubtful. As her eyes got bigger, she noticed the camera on her.

"You don't look so sure, Bree," Linley said.

"It's mostly amazement that Petra is confident we'll get this done." Briana put an arm around Petra. "The one thing I've learned over the last two days is to trust what Petra says."

"It looks like I could help the most by going out and making sure Chris gets in here." Linley paused a moment and then gave the hand signal to cut.

"OK, we'll do whatever it takes to get this finished. Suzanne and Anna are nearly finished, so I'll send one of them over here to help with the finishing and load-in. You can have Sebastian too. And I'm going to get Chris over here for real. He's been busy signing autographs out there."

Everyone laughed. Good thing Chris was good-natured. He took the brunt of everyone's teasing.

Once the bed was suspended, the work could move forward. They used a staple gun to put the carpet border all around the platform. They covered the top edge with a decorative brick-colored braid. Petra called it gimp, which spawned way too many "gimpy" jokes.

Most of the fun was like those puns, lighthearted and filled with teasing.

Who could have guessed what an unforgettable experience this would be? Briana had dreaded it for so long, it was hard to realize that she now hated to have it end.

Not that everything had changed. In fact, nothing had changed except her attitude. Her dad was still coming home, though she figured it would be long after the reveals. Her mom had sent Suzanne over here so she could stay and help the Harris team. That was another sign nothing had changed. Her mom still preferred to stay in her own safe place, to be there to make sure the elephant wasn't discovered.

I'm taking one day at a time—no—one moment at a time. For right now, I'm completely happy.

They managed to break for lunch, though nobody was taking a leisurely break. Briana got a sandwich and some fruit and sat down at one of the tables. Surely she didn't have to eat standing up.

"Hi, Briana." Her mother put her plate down next to Briana's. "Do you mind if I sit here?" Her mom seemed happy.

"Of course not." Briana finished chewing. "Thank you, Mom, for getting word to me last night. I figured it must have been hard for you to say that much to Sebastian."

"I knew how much you worried. I tried not to let on it was anything but a scheduling change."

"Well, thank you. It meant I got to sleep last night."

"Do you know what I got today?" Mom's smile said it was something special.

Briana just waited.

"Your brothers sent me flowers. Look at this note." She pushed a handwritten note over to Briana. Since it was in their handwriting, they had to have planned ahead and sent it to each other and then sent the note to the florist.

"Dear Mom," it read in Michael's handwriting, "Since Bree is getting a whole room makeover, we wanted you to have something beautiful as well. Thank you for your letters."

Then in Matt's handwriting it continued, "We realized how much we've missed you. We know things are not perfect at home, but we've stayed away too long. Plan on both of us for Christmas break this year." Both of them signed the letter.

"Oh, Mom!" Briana could hardly speak.

"If you hadn't told me you had written, I might not have begun to write to them. It was easy to pretend they were too busy to come home instead of facing the truth."

"Can you believe it? We'll all be together for Christmas!"

Her mom seemed a little quiet. "Honey, you know it might not be perfect."

What was it her prayer said? Something like "it is what it is." She squeezed her mom's hand. "We can count on it not being perfect, Mom—whether it's Dad or whether it's something else. I'm just beginning to see that I can sometimes be reasonably happy when everything is not perfect."

"Briana." It was Petra. "We better hit it."

"OK." Briana gave her mom a kiss on the cheek. "Thanks for helping me with this experience, Mom."

"It turned out to be just as much fun for me. I really learned a lot from Suzanne." She laughed. "I'm seeing new window treatments and linens throughout the house before Christmas."

The room really began to come together by late afternoon.

Linley came in at about three thirty with a clipboard stuck under her arm and an oversized brass pot filled with dried flowers. "Where do you want this, Petra?" The cameraman continued to film.

"Over there beside the desk."

"I can't believe you guys did this. It's like another world," Linley said.

"You doubted me after all this time?"

"I always doubt. My problem is that I always see all the stuff that needs to be done, not what's already under way."

"I'll tell you a secret." Petra spoke into the camera. "I worried this time as well. If I hadn't had this team"— she put her arm around Briana—"I never could have pulled this off."

"Great. Cut," Linley said.

"Everybody—I meant what I said about this team— though it's bigger than just Bree and me."

"I know," Briana said. "We rock!"

"Let me go over the last details," Linley said as she flipped a few pages on her clipboard. "You're still first on the schedule for everything. Petra, your designer's chat is at five. Everybody else, have something to drink in the kitchen."

Linley looked at the clipboard again. "Derek will bring Chickie over at five thirty for the reveal."

"Do we get to watch?" Briana asked.

"No. The footage on the designer's chats and your friend's reaction to the reveal is kept under wraps until the show airs," Linley said.

"Once I've finished over here, we'll head over to Briana's house. Designer chat at about six if we don't have any trouble here, with the reveal to follow, probably about six thirty."

"As you finish, start your pack-up, and we'll all meet for one last dinner at seven thirty, followed by a wrap up meeting."

"We're going to try to get out of here tonight?" Jack asked.

"If the film looks good. Take a quick look after the reveal. If anything goes wrong, we can spend one more night and reshoot any scenes in the morning; but so far, according to Derek, it's been flawless."

She turned to Sebastian. "You, Joe, and Chris finish packing the truck, OK? The canteen tent, tables, and chairs will go on last, after our wrap meeting."

"We're pretty close to being done already," Sebastian said, "since the carpentry projects finished a couple hours ago."

Linley covered a few more details and then left them to load in the rooms. Since starting this *Flip Flop* experience, Briana had become an old pro at the lingo. Load in meant moving all the furniture back into the room, hanging the window coverings, and putting on all the finishing touches.

As the room came together, Briana couldn't believe the overall look. It looked like a room from a sultan's palace—like something out of *Arabian Nights*. Mom and Suzanne had made a duvet cover out of one of the fabrics. It looked beautiful on the flying-carpet bed.

Pillows of every shape and color were stacked on the bed, some even made of a metallic gold lamé. Briana knew they'd have many a talk in the years to come swinging on Chickie's magic carpet.

"Come, look," Petra said. She stretched across the bed on her back and Briana joined her.

Briana knew the cameras were still rolling, but at this point she was used to them. She trusted that the crew would edit out any gross stuff.

"Look at the ceiling."

"Oh!" Briana was speechless. When the carpenters installed the crown molding, they'd left a gap between the molding and the ceiling for tube lighting to be installed invisibly. It now lit the ceiling. "It looks exactly like you described it. I can't believe we are not looking through a metal grate to a rosy glow in the sky."

"I imagined it," Petra said, "but I'm never sure I can really pull it off."

"Forget how Chickie will react . . . I think I'm going to cry."

Petra grabbed Briana's hand. "This has been a *Flip Flop* I'll never forget." She gave the hand a squeeze. "For a lot of reasons."

When the room was done, Briana wanted to stay. She couldn't get enough of the room. Petra finally had to shoo them all out so she could do the designer's chat with Linley.

Briana went down into the kitchen to wait for Derek or his assistant to take her over for her own reveal. She felt tired and happy. After everything that had happened over the last few days, her room hardly mattered—it would be icing on the cake. If she ended up with leopard spots on the walls, it would be worth it.

She looked at her watch. A little past six. If her dad had left first thing in the morning, he could be here anytime. Of course, depending on what he meant by relaxing last night, he might not have gotten an early start.

It was hard to know how she even felt about her dad. Seeing him during the B-roll shoot showed her a different man than the one who belittled and accused her. Maybe the reason Mom kept going is because she remembered that other man—the funny, sweet one. Maybe she thought the ugly one was only temporary. *The temporary one is almost the only one I can remember.*

Nothing has changed at home except my room. But I've changed. I'm still not sure how, but writing to my brothers, trying to talk to my mother—all those are drastic changes for me. Maybe that's the courage to change the things I can change.

She thought about her dad's drinking again. When she was little she used to think that if she was just good enough, or if she kept her room clean enough, or if she got high enough grades, her father wouldn't be so upset that he'd have to drink.

I've grown up since then. I do know it has nothing to do with me. It's an illness that only he can fight. Maybe that's the acceptance of things that cannot be changed.

She opened her bag and took out the framed prayer. "Reasonably happy in this life . . ." *Hmmm. Maybe that's what I've been trying to do when I tried to reconnect with Matt and Michael and Mom. Maybe when they come we just need to take a good hard look at the elephant in the living room together—even talk about it. Ignoring it is too full of secrecy.*

She thought about her help-me-Jesus prayers. *Weird.*

I was asking Him to help me keep it all secret, to allow me to keep living in my cave. Maybe Jesus was telling me that my Pandora's box was too big a burden.

She thought about what Petra and Sebastian had said. *Jesus, thank You. Instead of giving me what I asked for in order to keep living my fearful life, You gave me what I needed to live a reasonably happy life. Thank You. You know that Pandora's box I always talk about? I think that's the burden You talk about in the Bible. You knew. That burden made me more than weary. Sebastian had it right, Lord. I need to turn it over to You. In fact, there's no "need to" about it—*

"OK, Bree," Derek said as he walked into the kitchen. "Are you ready for your reveal?"

"Yes. I am." *Lord, I'm taking all my secrets, all my fears about my dad—my whole Pandora's box—and I'm giving it to You.*

"You're quiet," Derek said as they walked across the greenbelt. "Are you nervous?"

"No. I'm so sorry to see this experience end. You have no idea what it's meant to me."

He smiled.

As she got closer to the house, she saw her dad's car in the driveway. Her stomach clenched automatically. *Lord, You can have the elephant as well.*

She met Linley outside her bedroom.

"Close your eyes and hold my hand as we move into the room. You're going to want to move all around the room to see, but the camera would only catch your backside if you did that. Try to take in the room, one piece at a time from your vantage place." Linley paused. "I'll highlight things for you."

"OK."

"Ready?"

"Yes."

Briana closed her eyes and let Linley lead her into the room. It had a fresh paint smell, and she could catch the scent of candles burning—vanilla?

"You told us you were tired of your cave—that you wanted a room filled with light and fresh air. Open your eyes."

Briana opened her eyes to a room bathed in light. Her hardwood floor remained the same, but everything else was different.

"Claire and Chickie decided to take you at your word," Linley said. "You have five different shades of paint in here, from the palest cream to a soft café au lait."

"I love it! It's everything I could have wanted." Briana didn't mean to, but tears began slipping down her cheeks. The room represented all that had taken place in her life. She had left her cave of secrets and moved into the light.

"Look around the top of the walls, between that gorgeous crown molding and the molding below. Claire lettered words that run all the way around your room."

Briana looked up. There, in Claire's artistic lettering, were the first four lines of the "Serenity Prayer"—one line on every wall, each line separated by a subtle leaf design. The lettering was in the beige color, so it didn't stand out in the room.

"It's beautiful—all shadings and etchings."

Her furniture had been painted with a shabby chic look. "I love the furniture."

"They painted it the darkest beige first, then white over it; then Chickie carefully sanded off part of the white to reveal the darker paint."

"It makes it look like it's been like that forever." Briana thought she probably sounded like an idiot. She didn't have enough words to express how she felt.

Linley pointed out the armoire they'd made for her. When the doors opened, it revealed a computer desk with file drawers and storage compartments.

They'd created a new headboard that matched the armoire. The bed linens repeated all the subtle shadings of the paint. She had at least as many pillows as Chickie had.

She could see the exact place on the wall where her gift from Petra would go.

"I love this room. It rocks!"

"One more quirky thing," Linley said. "See over here on the floor? Something had scratched deep grooves in the floor. They were evenly spaced, but deep gouges."

Briana knew exactly what they were. Those were the hash marks she gouged into the floor each time she made it through another one of the nightmares with Dad.

"Chris suggested we replace those boards, but Claire refused. She got down on the floor and painted each groove in an alternating color. Isn't it surprisingly beautiful?"

The tears filled Briana's eyes again. She couldn't speak.

"Claire says it reminds her of an Amish quilt. The quilter always allows at least one mistake to remain in the quilt pattern." Linley smiled. "The quilter believes it keeps her from getting prideful, but Claire says it represents life." Linley paused. "She says that when the design is finished, it's often the deepest wounds that yield the greatest beauty."

If they didn't cut soon, Briana knew she'd be a blubbering mess. She loved her room. She loved what the room revealed about Claire's heart, but she could see the hand of the Heavenly Designer as well.

Chickie came in and everything was a blur. They hugged and cried.

Linley signed off with those familiar words, "That does it for Mercey Springs and another episode of *Flip Flop. . . .*"

As the cameras stopped and everyone talked at once, Briana looked down at the grooved design on the floor. *OK, I get it, Lord. I will treasure that message from You forever.*

As they all walked out to the greenbelt for dinner and the wrap-up, she noticed her father's car was gone. She knew it could only mean one thing.

Derek

stood up by the barbeque. "OK, everyone, we've looked at much of the footage, and I want to announce that it's a wrap. We've got our show."

Everyone clapped, Sebastian and Joe whistled, and Chickie grabbed Briana and hugged her.

"We want to thank Chickie and Bree—wait till you see yourselves on television. The camera loved you both. I also want to thank our local assistants. I ought to be giving out awards, but these checks will have to do. Anna, you did a wonderful job. Suzanne said she wants to take you with us to our next location."

"Nick, Trish, and Geoff, we loved the food here. You spoiled us totally. We're banning scales for the next ten days."

"Sebastian, if you ever want a permanent job and are willing to travel, you've got an open offer. We decided it was a good thing the camera never saw you, or Carpenter Chris would be looking over his shoulder."

"Our team did it again. This will be one of the top shows. You girls will be seeing your seventeen-year-old selves in rerun when you have little kids running around your knees."

He pointed at both Petra and Claire. "You outdid yourselves on the designs this time. I'm guessing there'll be a run on magic-carpet beds."

"Anyway, thank you, everyone. Mercey Springs was a huge success. If we can get Nick to offer his prayer again, we can eat."

Nick prayed for everyone for the last time and then invited everyone to fill up their plates.

Briana went over to her mom as she stood near the back of the group. "I saw Dad's car."

Mom sighed. "He was tired from driving so long, and there was so much confusion, he decided to just get out of the way."

"I'm sorry, Mom," Briana said. "Are you worrying about when he comes back?"

"Yes. He's definitely in a mood. I think he feels left out. I tried to make him . . . well, you know."

"Yep. It's not your fault, Mom, and there's not a single thing we can do about it."

"Well, I'm going to try to listen for his car and see if I

can't head him off so he doesn't come out here." Mom grimaced. "With the sewing center all packed up and his garage and house back to normal, maybe he'll be happier."

"I don't mean to be judging Dad; I'm just observing, but I don't think there's a thing we can do to change Dad's mind when he feels he needs to drink. I used to make myself crazy trying to do the right thing so he wouldn't get mad at me."

"Let's try to enjoy the rest of the evening. I had such fun with Suzanne and with Nick and Trish that I'm feeling a little resentful toward anything that threatens to steal the enjoyment."

Briana raised an eyebrow but said nothing. That was a first. Her mom always did everything to make Dad happy. She couldn't remember her mother ever talking about her own enjoyment.

"Hurry up, Bree," Chickie said, coming up behind her. "Get your plate and join Joe, Sebastian, and me. I want to hear everything."

I'm going to be like Mom tonight. I'll listen for Dad, but I want this night to last as long as it can.

She sat down with Chickie and the boys and then waved to Petra and Claire to come over. She'd come to love Petra in the time they were together. And Claire! She needed to thank her for the room. What an experience.

They laughed and talked, telling stories and teasing each other until Derek called for them to load the tables and chairs and head out.

How they all hated to say good-bye to Joe. He and Chris would drive the truck up to Napa Valley, where they were to film the next show.

Just as the truck drove out, Briana heard shouting from the direction of her house. *Oh, no! Dad.*

"Stay here," Petra whispered. "Let me go." She went over to the barbecue and picked up an extra plate of food and headed toward Bree's dad.

"Look, Bree," Chickie said. "Your dad's home. I think he's waving good-bye to the truck."

Briana didn't say anything. Despite all her new-found resolve, there was nothing she hated more than a scene.

"Petra's going over to bring him food. Maybe he'll come and join us." Chickie still didn't get it. "We should go and get some of our own chairs."

Briana looked at Sebastian, and she could see that he'd figured out something was wrong. He didn't say anything, though. He just reached down and squeezed her hand.

"He's probably tired from the long drive," she heard herself saying. "I'm sure he'll probably go home and crash." *Why am I lying again?* "Thanks anyway, Chickie."

As they talked with Claire, she watched Petra talk to her father and put an arm around him. Mom came up and the three of them walked back toward the house.

Briana watched until she saw Petra coming back.

"It was good to be able to see your dad one last time, Bree. He's exhausted and sends his regrets that he can't come out and play with us."

Briana sent Petra a look of gratitude. Later when Briana walked her to the car, Petra said, "Every look you've sent me is filled with your undying gratitude."

Briana laughed. "Oh, you read me so well."

"No need to be indebted, my friend. It was easy. Years of practice taught me the art of distraction." Petra gave her a hug. "I feel as if I've made a friend, Bree. May God continue to make Himself real to you."

"Thank you, Petra. Now I know why God didn't answer my prayer when I begged Him not to pick us for *Flip Flop*. I wanted Him to let me keep my secrets. I had an iron grip, hanging on to all my problems. If I'd been listening to Him, I could've probably heard Him saying, 'Let go. Let go. What I've got for you is so much better than what you are trying to hang on to.'"

Petra laughed. "Boy, is that the story of my life."

"One of the wonderful things He had for me was you. I will never forget you, Petra."

The hugs and good-byes went on for more than a half hour. When the final car pulled away, Briana felt like an important chapter in her life closed. Of course, when one chapter is finished, another is just beginning.

"Tonight," Chickie announced, "I'm going to take a magic carpet ride to the land of nod."

"Me too. I mean, I'm going to bed—not as exotic but just as needed," Briana said.

"I'd ask you to spend the night, but I know we're both dying to experience our own rooms."

"I'll be over first thing in the morning. We've got so much to catch up on."

"Tomorrow night will be a slumber party at my house, the following night, your room."

My room. Hmmmm. There's definitely no getting everything back into Pandora's box. In fact, the whole thing had been given to the Lord, so it was His problem. *I just know I don't want to live a lie anymore. I want to live as if I have nothing to hide.*

Good morning, Bree," Chickie's father sat at the breakfast table. "I don't know what I'm going to do now that I only have five to cook for. You will take pity on me and stay for breakfast, won't you?"

"If you put it that way . . ." Briana had missed being part of the Wells family during the last few crazy days. "After we eat breakfast, I fully intend to help you clean up all the debris left from our canteen."

"I'll not be turning you down on that one."

"Is Chickie still sleeping?"

"We haven't seen her yet. I sort of wondered if she had any seasickness last night, but I didn't have the heart to wake her to see. Why don't you go up there and roust her out of bed?"

"Cool. I haven't gotten to torture her in two days."

Briana found Chickie lying on her bed looking at the ceiling.

"Can I tell you how much I love this room? I feel as if I'm in a different world."

Briana climbed onto the platform, joining her on the magic carpet.

"Your dad was wondering if you got seasick last night."

"No. It's a gentle rocking, almost like a cradle. Yeah, that's it," she said, laughing. "I slept like a baby."

"Look up. Can't you almost picture the warmth growing as the sun rises higher in the sky?" Chickie added.

"So you do love it, then."

"It's so beyond what I pictured. I guess I hoped for a headboard and bedspread and new paint."

"You know you can never change your room. People will be talking about it for years to come—the famous Moroccan-Sunrise bedroom. One hundred years from now, when someone sells the house, they'll still be talking Moroccan Sunrise."

"Oh, how I've missed you, Bree." Chickie hung her leg over the bed, causing a gentle movement. "I guess I should be happy that we don't get earthquakes here in the Central Valley. Can you imagine my flying carpet in a seven-point-oh earthquake?"

"I love my room as well. I feel as if it marks a new life for me—open and fresh." Briana knew Chickie would understand later. "Your dad's cooking breakfast. Let's go down and feed our faces. I got mighty used to his cooking."

The whole family was seated and eating French toast when the girls came down.

"We wondered if you were hoping for slaves from the sultan's household to bring breakfast up to you." Sebastian looked rested. His sense of humor hadn't left.

"Are you applying for the job?" Chickie said as she took two slices off the griddle.

"Only if you pay me as much as I made from *Flip Flop*."

"It wasn't bad, huh?" Briana asked.

"In a little more than four days, with the bonus that Derek gave me, I made as much as I could have made working the whole summer at Mickey D's."

"We couldn't believe our check either," Mr. Wells said. "I felt as if I should've told him we'd have been happy to do it for free."

"Chickie, I think the experience was the best I've ever had. It sounds like everyone agrees. Thank you for applying and forcing me to follow through," said Briana.

"Can I be excused?" Geoff asked. "I want to do my trash pickup of the greenbelt so I can get my money too."

"Sure," Mrs. Wells said. "Take one of those big green trash bags with you."

After he left, Sebastian stood up to leave.

"Sebastian, will you wait just a minute?" Suddenly Briana felt shy. "I have something I wanted to share with you."

"With me?" Sebastian asked.

"No, I mean, with all of you."

Sebastian sat back down.

"I haven't been completely honest with you." She looked around the table. "No, I've actually been deceiving you and covering things up to keep you from knowing the truth about me."

No one said anything, but Mr. Wells got up and refilled her orange juice glass.

"Haven't you wondered, Chickie, why I'm always over here and never invite you to my house?"

Chickie waited for her to continue.

"And didn't it seem strange that my brothers left and never came back?" She paused. "Don't I often seem distracted or tense?"

Sebastian nodded his head. He must have been thinking about last night.

"I've spent my whole life with secrets, and I want to trust my story to a few close friends. Here's what I'm trying to say: My father is an alcoholic. He doesn't drink at work and is well respected on the job; but when he comes home, he unwinds. We never know when he'll come home drunk."

No one moved around the table.

"When he drinks he becomes verbally abusive, and it often goes on most of the night. He's never hurt us physically, though." Bree felt relieved to get the words out.

"I have to say, Bree, that I suspected something like this," Mr. Wells said. "Matt once came close to saying something—asking us to watch out for you."

"He did?"

"Not in so many words, but I understood. Do you know how many years I've prayed for you and your family? I'm not going to stop now."

"After this last week, I knew I couldn't go back to my cave—and I don't mean my room—I mean my hidey-hole of secrets." She looked at Chickie. Would Chickie forgive her for keeping secrets for so long? Her friend's head was still down. Chickie couldn't meet her eyes.

"I'm so sorry, Chickie, for keeping this secret. You kept saying you knew everything about me, and I let you go on thinking that. Will you forgive me?"

Chickie looked up, tears on her cheeks. "Me forgive you? Are you kidding? You were in all that pain and I never figured it out? What kind of friend am I?"

"Listen," Mrs. Wells said. "I don't think any of us should feel bad. It takes time to learn to reveal ourselves. I think you made a big step today."

"What big step did you make today, Briana?" Her mother stood in the door of the kitchen. "Oh, hi, everyone. I came over to help you with the cleanup, Trish."

"Hi, Mom."

"So what step did you make . . . besides using a sewing machine for the very first time?" her mom said, laughing.

"I told them about Dad."

The smile faded from her mother's face. "I need to go. Please excuse me." She turned and walked out the door.

"My mom feels that our problems need to be kept private. She'll be very upset with me." Briana stood up. "Thank you for being such good friends."

"Do you want me to walk you home?" Sebastian asked.

"Thank you, but no. I don't want to cause Mom any more upset by having someone else present." She started to leave. "My mother so enjoyed being with you. I hope your knowing won't change your offer of friendship. She needs friends."

As she walked home, she worried about whether she'd made the right choice. After all, it was her father's story, and she shared it. But it was her story too. And by covering it up, she had to lie too many times. *Lord, help me know what's right.*

She walked into the kitchen and saw her mother sitting at the table, hands clenched together. "You told."

"Mom, I can't keep lying."

"I worked so hard to keep anyone from knowing. . . ."

"But, Mom, when trusted friends know, we have someone to pray for us."

"I just don't know if I can go on if everyone knows. The only way I keep going is by refusing to give in to it."

"I don't know what's right, but I do know that by never talking about this, we've driven a wedge in our whole family. We're just now getting ready to talk openly with you—the boys and me. It's so important."

"I don't know. I just don't know."

They sat together silently for a time before Mom spoke again. "Maybe you're right. I do know that doing things my way hasn't made anything better."

"Mom, I wish you'd start going to church with me. That's made all the difference."

"Maybe sometime . . ."

As they sat, someone knocked at the back door and then came in.

"Anna, can you come to town with me to return the rented barbecue?" Chickie's mom seemed her old self.

Briana was sure her mom would say no when she got up and said, "Sure. I think I can use a long talk."

"Well, then, I'm going over to help everyone else clean up," Briana said.

"We'll talk more later," her mom said.

Something in her voice told Briana that she meant it.

Geoff, move away from the Christmas tree. If you scoot back any more, you'll end up toppling the whole thing." Mrs. Wells carried a tray of Christmas goodies and put them on the coffee table.

"But it's so crowded in here," Geoff whined.

"If it feels too crowded to you, go upstairs and read a book. We're here to watch our famous sisters in rerun." Sebastian tossed soft drink cans to Matt and Michael.

"My dorm had a special Chickie and Bree fan night when the episode aired for the first time," Matt said, pulling on his sister's hair. "I could have made a nice tidy sum selling the two phone numbers."

"Stop teasing," Briana said. "You've only been here a few days, and I'm already remembering what it was like to have two big brothers."

"So, you missed us?" Michael asked, his voice holding the same teasing tone as his brother's.

Briana looked around the room to see the whole Wells family—her second family—and her mom and two brothers. What more could she want? "I hate to admit it, but I did miss the two of you. Of course, Sebastian is almost as bad as you guys, so I've still had my share of teasing."

Mom stood up to get more drinks from the kitchen. "Trish, do you need me to run back home and get more drinks and snacks?"

"No. I think we'll be OK. I'm sending the whole crew over to you tomorrow, so save your groceries for then."

"Will Brian be home tonight?" Mr. Wells asked.

"Yes, supposedly. He's driving in from the airport. I left him a note, so he may be over, but who knows."

Briana's family had come a long way. Her brothers were home for Christmas break, and her mom had made a decision to no longer cover up the choices made by Briana's dad.

And Dad—that remained a complicated thing. Sometimes Briana felt that he was making progress. Briana tried to reach out to him when he was home and sober. But he still hadn't conquered his alcoholism, even though he'd talked about getting help. Ever since she and her mom decided to leave when he started ranting, it seemed to take the wind out of his fury.

Sometimes both of them would end up over at the Wells house—Mom on the couch and Briana on the flying carpet with Chickie. Mom and Chickie's mom had become good friends.

At first the Wells family prayed for Dad and the whole Harris family, but pretty soon Mom was attending church too; and now Mom and Briana were praying too. *Weird. Good weird, though.*

When the boys arrived, they and Briana had a great visit and talked long into the night—getting everything out in the open. Briana shared her "Serenity Prayer." Matt and Michael loved it as well. For Christmas, Briana had color photocopies made of the hand-lettered prayer and had them framed for Mom, Michael, and Matt. Just a couple of days ago it hit her: Why not make one for Dad as well? Just as it was important not to deny his alcoholism, she decided she couldn't shut him out of her life either.

One thing Michael said really stuck with her. After he finished reading the prayer, he reread the words, "reasonably happy."

"That's how I'm going to look at it," he had said. "We may not be perfect, but we can all work at being a reasonably happy family."

"Earth to Bree. Earth to Bree." Chickie pulled her back to the present.

"Where she goes, I'll never know," Sebastian said.

"And I'll never tell." Briana shifted the pillow that separated her back from the wood of the coffee table.

"Shhh," Mr. Wells said, "here we go."

The opening credits began to roll for *Flip Flop*. Briana's grimace was the biggest image on the screen. Derek had said that the camera loved her, but she'd never expected her off-the-wall expressions to be part of the opening credits on every show and every promo and commercial. Of course, Chickie showed up plenty too. Briana wondered how many girls tried to replicate Chickie's hair color.

"So, Briana," Michael asked, "how does it feel to have your face appear in millions of homes all across America every single week?"

"All I can say is that it's a good thing I don't have any secrets."

Daughters of the Faith series, for ages 8-12

A story based on the life of holocaust survivor, Anita Dittman.

Shadow of His Hand
ISBN: 0-8024-4074-6

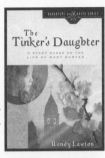

A story based on the life of Mary Bunyan, the daughter of John Bunyan.

The Tinker's Daughter
ISBN: 0-8024-4099-1

A story based on the life of Mary Chilton, a young girl from Holland who traveled to America on the Mayflower.

Almost Home
ISBN: 0-8024-3637-4

A story based on the life of Pioneer Olive Oatman.

Ransom's Mark
ISBN: 0-8024-3638-2

A story based on the life of Harriet Tubman, who was freed from slavery through the Underground Railroad.

Courage to Run
ISBN: 0-8024-4098-3

A story based on the life of Salvation Army Pioneer Eliza Shirley.

The Hallelujah Lass
ISBN: 0-8024-4073-8

FLIP FLOP TEAM

ACQUIRING EDITOR
Michele Straubel

COPY EDITOR
Cessandra Dillon

BACK COVER COPY
Becky Armstrong

COVER DESIGN
UDG DesignWorks, Inc.

COVER PHOTO
Steve Gardner/pixelworksstudio.net

INTERIOR DESIGN
Ragont Design

PRINTING AND BINDING
Bethany Press International

The typeface for the text of this book is
Giovanni